CARTEL KILLAZ 2

Lock Down Publications and Ca$h
Presents
Cartel Killaz 2
A Novel by *Hood Rich*

Lock Down Publications
P.O. Box 870494
Mesquite, Tx 75187

Visit our website @
www.lockdownpublications.com

Copyright 2019 by Hood Rich
CARTEL KILLAZ 2

First Edition November 2019
Printed in the United States of America

This is a work of fiction. Names, characters, places, and incidents either are products of the author's imagination or are used fictitiously. Any similarity to actual events or locales or persons, living or dead, is entirely coincidental.

Lock Down Publications
Like our page on Facebook: Lock Down Publications @
www.facebook.com/lockdownpublications.ldp
Cover design and layout by: **Dynasty Cover Me**
Book interior design by: **Shawn Walker**
Edited by: **Jill Duska**

Stay Connected with Us!

Text **LOCKDOWN** to 22828 to stay up-to-date with new releases, sneak peaks, contests and more…

Thank you.

Submission Guideline.

Submit the first three chapters of your completed manuscript to ldpsubmissions@gmail.com, subject line: Your book's title. The manuscript must be in a .doc file and sent as an attachment. Document should be in Times New Roman, double spaced and in size 12 font. Also, provide your synopsis and full contact information. If sending multiple submissions, they must each be in a separate email.

Have a story but no way to send it electronically? You can still submit to LDP/Ca$h Presents. Send in the first three chapters, written or typed, of your completed manuscript to:

LDP: Submissions Dept
Po Box 870494
Mesquite, Tx 75187

DO NOT send original manuscript. Must be a duplicate.

Provide your synopsis and a cover letter containing your full contact information.

Thanks for considering LDP and Ca$h Presents.

Hood Rich

Chapter 1

Prentice fell backward, busting his gun over and over again. It roared in the basement. He kept his sights directly on Keisha and tried his best to knock her out of the game. He hated her for crossing him. He hated her for getting pregnant by his cousin, Mudman, and for carrying on in his face about it as if it were no big deal. He watched one of his slugs land in Keisha's left shoulder.

She screamed as the bullet threw her backward.

Prentice smiled and aimed toward her fallen body. He closed his right eye and bit into his bottom lip, ready to fill her with holes. Before he could, she jumped up and flew over the back of the couch, landing hard. "Shit!" she groaned.

Prentice didn't waste any more time. He got to bucking at the couch, trying to chop through it. Big holes filled the sofa. It smelled like gunpowder and burnt cloth in the basement. "Punk-ass bitch!" he hollered.

"Rome, help me!" Keisha screamed, calling Mudman by his government name. She laid flat on her stomach and covered her head with her right arm.

Mudman stood there in disbelief. He couldn't fathom what he was witnessing. He was so taken aback that he'd been frozen in place. When he heard Keisha call his name, he snapped out of it. He knelt down and grabbed his .40 from the side of the chair he'd been sitting in. He cocked the hammer and aimed the gun at Prentice. Before he could even think about the consequences of busting at his cousin, he squeezed the trigger twice. Shells leaped out of the gun and both of the slugs slammed into Prentice's back and turned him around.

"Ahh!" Prentice turned right around and busted his gun three times. All three slugs hit up Mudman, two to the chest, and one to the arm.

Mudman felt the hot lead rock his vest. The steel burned through the armor and singed the skin of his body. It felt like he was being poked by a flaming sword. The round to his arm started to bleed like crazy. The bullet had knocked a nice chunk out of him. He gritted his teeth and rushed Prentice at full speed, bleeding. He pressed his barrel right to him, and finger fucked his trigger. Bright lights from the fire of the gun flashed over and over again.

Prentice leaped onto his tippy toes four times. His eyes were bucked as he felt the bullets ripping through him. His knees went weak. He tried to raise his gun. "You bitch-ass nigga. I - "

Boom! Boom! Boom!

Bullets hit up Prentice's side, knocking him sideways. He was so hopped up on heroin and Percocets that he could barely feel the pain of the rounds. Prentice turned around and saw the smoking gun in Keisha's hands. His eyes got as big as saucers. She fired two more shots. He flew backward, stunned. He fell on his back. Keisha stood over him with the smoking gun. Tears rolled down her cheeks. Blood oozed out of her shoulder. She stepped over Prentice and looked down on him with blurred vision because of her crying. "I hate you, Prentice. I hate you for what you did to my sister. I'll never forgive you. Never!" She dropped the gun and cried into her hands.

Mudman hopped over the fallen Prentice and pulled her into his embrace. "Shawty. Shawty, come on now. It's all over. He dead, look at him," Mudman assured her. He glanced down at the unmoving body of his cousin.

Keisha came out of his embrace and looked down at Prentice. She felt no mercy. She hoped he rotted in hell. She hugged Mudman again. "We gotta get out of here, baby. I know somebody heard those gunshots. We gotta get out of here before we wind up in jail."

Mudman agreed. He looked down at Prentice again. He felt a twinge of remorse for what had become of him, but then he felt the stinging pain of his gunshot wounds. Had he not been so hopped up on painkillers himself, he would have been in extreme agony like Keisha was in because of her shoulder.

"A'ight, Shawty, let's get the fuck out of hurr." He tucked his pistol and rushed to the back of the basement, where he kept one of his many safes. He entered the combination and opened it.

Keisha took a sheet from the dryer and wrapped it around her arm. She tied it as tight as she could and winced in pain. "We gotta get the fuck out of here," she mumbled.

"I know, baby. I'm almost done hurr." Mudman took the cash and stuffed all of it into his duffel bag. Next came the bricks of the Sinaloa Tar.

"Hurry up." Keisha could swear that she heard sirens somewhere off in the distance. She felt nervous and afraid. On top of that, she was in excruciating pain. She was already thinking about making it to her mother's home. Kimmie was a certified nurse. She kept a lot of first aid stuff at her home. She knew her mother would have no problem getting the bullets out of them and sewing them up, assuming they didn't lose too much blood.

Mudman suddenly felt woozy. The bullet wounds brought forth stinging pains that felt like torture. He fought through it and stuffed the last bit of work into his duffel bag. He zipped it up and turned around to face Keisha. But what he saw nearly made him lose all of his breath.

Prentice sat up with blood leaking out of him. He smiled sinisterly at Keisha and shot her twice in the stomach purposely. "Punk bitch."

She screamed and fell over the couch.

Mudman hollered. "Noooo!" He rushed Prentice and fired another round, hitting Prentice directly in the chest. Prentice flew on to his back and closed his eyes.

Mudman knelt beside Keisha. He picked her up into his warm embrace. She was a bloody mess. "Baby, please, fight. Fight, baby, please."

Keisha's eyes rolled into the back of her head. She was in so much pain that her body began to shut down. Her tongue blocked her airway. She started to shake. Blood filled Mudman's lap quickly.

"Aw shit! Keisha! Come on, baby! Fuck!"

She was shaking so bad that he could barely contain her. She coughed, and blood came out of her mouth. It spilled down the side of her cheek. "Arrgh!"

Mudman tried to contain her. He laid her out on her back. She continued to shake. "Fuck, what do I do?" he hollered.

Keisha stopped shaking. She lay on the floor stretched out, unmoving. Blood spilled out of her shoulder and stomach wounds. A small puddle appeared around her.

Mudman heard sirens getting closer. He didn't know if they were coming for them or for someone else, but he was starting to panic. He had always been told that when a person was shot, you weren't supposed to move them from fear that the bullet could start to move around and damage vital organs. Also, that constant movement caused a person to bleed more profusely. But he didn't give a fuck. He had to get Keisha out of that basement. There was no way that he could ever leave her behind. He ran over and grabbed his duffel bag full of money and Sinaloa Tar. Then he picked Keisha up and rushed out of the back door with her. He was thankful that earlier that day something had told him to park in the back garage of the house, which was connected to an alley. With his injuries and the heavy weight of his bleeding woman, it almost overwhelmed his physical capabilities to handle everything, but somehow, and some way, he was able to get her into the back seat of his truck. He laid her out the long way, before getting into the driver's seat, woozier than he ever remembered being. He started the ignition and stepped on the gas.

The truck peeled out of the garage with its wheels spinning. Mudman stormed down the alley just as two police cars came storming past the street he was about to enter. They saw his truck and came to a screeching halt. Mudman slammed on the brakes and threw the truck in reverse. He flew backward at forty miles an hour and slammed on the brakes again. Keisha fell on the floor of the truck with a loud thump. Then he was peeling out of the alley's alternative exit. He made a hard right on to the residential street. The truck fishtailed before straightening out. He sped down it and made a left onto a busy intersection. He took it for a mile at top speed. When he got to the expressway, he got on it, feeling dizzy and lightheaded. The truck swerved erratically.

"I got you, Keisha. I swear I do." He struggled to keep his eyes open as he drove. "I gotta get my baby to da hospital. I gotta..." His eyes lowered.

Cars beeped their horns. He jarred awake. He grabbed his cell phone and sent Figgady a text. When he looked up again, he sideswiped a car and swerved into the left lane, smashing into the back of a Nissan. His eyes grew heavier. He drove across two lanes and slapped another car before bullying his way off of the exit with his front bumper hanging off of the truck. When he got to the light, he could no longer keep his eyes open. They closed. His head hit the steering wheel, emitting the screaming of the horn, and then his truck was rolling into traffic.

Chapter 2
A year later...

Keisha stepped on the gas and took the black on black Hellcat to a hundred miles an hour. She bit into her bottom lip and smiled over at Mudman. "Dis what I needed right hurr, Rome. Dis shit got me feeling so alive!" She hollered, switched gears, and stepped on the gas again. The Hellcat shot forward and flew past the other cars on the highway. A constant zipping sound emitted as she passed each vehicle. She had a big smile on her face. Her pupils were dilated from the Mollie coursing through her system.

Mudman adjusted the Draco on his lap. He scanned the highway and pulled down the sun visor to block the harmful rays of the sun. He liked hearing and seeing that Keisha was finally coming out of her slump. After they'd gotten the news that the bullets had taken the life of their unborn child, Keisha had shut down for the better part of nine months. Mudman couldn't recall her uttering more than a paragraph during that span of time. The time had been a rough one for them. But they had gotten through it, and he felt that they'd come from under it two times stronger.

"Shawty, you already know dese ma'fuckas out hurr in Oakland got dem damn Helicopters and thangs. You betta slow yo' ass down." He looked into the rearview mirror to see if he could spot any highway patrolman.

They'd been laying low in Oakland for five months after setting Baton Rouge on fire. Figgady reported that the police were still back hole knocking on doors and asking questions about both Mudman and Keisha. That worried Mudman. He felt that he was able to handle his side of things when it came to the law, but to think that they were also looking for Keisha to probably put her behind bars, That spooked him, especially because he wasn't entirely sure of the reason they were looking for the pair. Figgady had been afraid to inquire.

"Shawty, you heard what the fuck I said?"

Keisha shook her head hard. "Fuck dat. I wish I could push dis bitch to a thousand miles an hour. I would. Whoo!" She punched the gas and took it to its maximum limit. Her hair flew and danced in the wind. The wind coursed over her face and made her feel alive again.

Finding out that she was no longer with child was devastating news for her to hear, so much so that she completely broke down and lost herself for nearly a year. On top of that mental anguish, she was remorseful for the fact that she'd taken Prentice's life. She could still remember how he looked with his body riddled with bullets, bullets that she'd put into him along with Mudman. Sometimes she regretted fucking with Mudman behind Prentice's back. After all, he was his cousin. Real women, she felt, didn't get down like that. Deep down she struggled with a dark conscience knowing that all of the problems that had taken place over the last two years had been her fault. Had she never succumbed to Mudman's courting, so many people would still have their lives, her little sister Kayla being one of them. The thought of Kayla caused her to shudder. She switched lanes and looked over to Mudman as he slipped a pair of Chanel sunglasses over his eyes. He was so fine to her. Over the time that they had been together, she had become downright obsessed with her man. She was sure he felt the same way about her. That made her smile.

Mudman glanced over at Keisha. He peeped her peeping him. He smiled for a second, and then his face turned serious. "A'ight, shawty, take yo' ma'fuckin' foot off that petal. The police detector just beeped. That means the law up hurr somewhere." He leaned his seat back. His eyes continued to scan the highway.

Keisha eased up off of the gas, as much as she hated to do it. She knew that her fun was over for now. "Baby, we gotta get into somethin' tonight. I'm bored as hell. I wanna get out." She waited until the speedometer hit seventy and clicked on the cruise control. In less than two seconds they rolled past two highway patrolmen. Keisha breathed a sigh of relief.

Mudman ducked lower. Not only was he wanted in Baton Rouge for absconding from his parole, but he was the prime suspect in multiple murders throughout the city as well. "Shawty, you already know I gotta meet up with Payroll tonight. He got a lick that I need to be a part of. We can't go on living in them damn Acorn Projects forever. It's some fuck nigga dat's around there that I just ain't feeling. Sooner or later I'ma have to take a good look at they ass. Ya feel me?"

Keisha nodded. She didn't like living in the projects either, but after they came from Baton Rouge with so much heat on them, the Acorn Projects seemed like their best stop, especially since the Oakland Police department was already under-manned by sixty percent. The remaining forty percent of the police officers that were available tended to stay away from the Acorn Projects for fear of losing their lives. Though Keisha hated the area, she was sure that she would hate prison even more.

"A'ight den, Mudman, you do what you gotta do. Just remember that I hate being in that apartment though. Dem niggas be shooting all in the hallway. Dis morning when I went out to go to the store they had two dead bodies shot up on the stairwell. People were going up and down the stairs like there wasn't nothing wrong with the sights before dem."

Mudman smiled at that. He loved that killer type of shit. Since he'd been in Oakland, he'd seen some of the most sadistic shit he'd ever witnessed in his entire life. It fascinated him. He knew that he was surrounded by lethal killers, and that excited him to no avail. "Baby, you ain't supposed to be leaving out of the fuckin' house no way when I ain't wit you. You already know what we up against. We gon' give dese Oakland niggas a run for they money, trust dat shit durr."

"When Figgady n'em supposed to be touching down?" Keisha asked, rolling off of the highway and stopping at a red light. She felt a twinge of pain in her stomach. Every now and then she would be reminded of the slugs that she'd received from Prentice.

"Soon as I buss a few moves and get my money right, I'ma send for my niggas. For right now, I'ma jam wit' yo' sister's baby daddy. Dat nigga seem like he got dese hurr streets figures out."

Keisha nodded. "Payroll a good nigga. He reminds me a lot of you. He crazy wit' dem hammers, and he don't let a I get away wit' nothing. Dat's probably why you taking to him so easily." Keisha pulled back off into traffic. She imagined the night she had ahead and grew depressed. She hated being cooped up in the apartment all the time. "Rome, would you mind if I stepped out tonight with Charity? We might go to a movie or catch a drink. I just don't wanna be sitting in that fuckin' house all night. It's making me start to get depressed all over again." She looked him over from the corner of her eyes.

Mudman shook his head. "Shawty, fuck all dat depression shit. Look, if you wanna step out tonight wit' Charity, dat shit cool wit' me. Just be careful. Any one of dem crazy niggas run up on you, you bet' not hesitate to blast dey ass. Trust me, after you kill somebody the first time, every other kill after that is easy. You hear me?"

Keisha nodded. "I ain't worried about shit. A I wanna they can damn sho' get it. I know where we at, trust and believe that." She took her .40 Glock from under her seat and set it on her lap. The weight of it caused her skirt to ride up on her thick thighs. They looked good to Mudman.

"Shawty, I don't give a fuck what you do tonight, but when I get home, you finna let a nigga fuck that big ole ass. I wanna hit that shit hard too. You wit' me on dat?" He reached under her skirt and rubbed her pussy through her panties. He could feel the weight of the gun resting on the back of it.

Keisha spaced her thighs. She took the gun and set it on the console of the Hellcat. She pulled her panties to the side. "Go on get you some of dat shit right there, Rome." Her fingers breezed through her pussy lips.

To the right of them was the Pacific Ocean. The beach surrounding it was massive. There looked like more than a hundred people already out getting ready to go for a swim. Keisha searched the parking lot for a space to park. She wanted to be able to enjoy Mudman's expert tongue on her clit. His tongue along with his dick game had been the reason it had been so easy for her to cross over to him, even while she was still involved with his cousin, Prentice.

Mudman opened the lips of her pussy and slid two fingers into her warmth. She felt tight. Her muscles squeezed around his digits almost immediately. In a matter of seconds, he was running them in and out of her. Her pussy got wetter and wetter. "You want me to tame dis pussy, huh?"

Keisha shivered and made a right into the big parking lot. "Yeah, baby. Please. Eat dis pussy." She placed her right foot on her seat and rested her knee against him.

Mudman lowered the Draco. He scooted all the way over= and sniffed her box. Her scent drifted up his nose. He groaned, placed his mouth over her lips, and began to eat her kat like a savage, holding her lips wide open, exposing her pink.

"Unn. Shit. Mudman," Keisha whispered. She pulled into a parking space and parked crooked. She hit the switch so that the roof raised on the car. As soon as it did, she locked her driver's door, rested against it, and cocked her thighs wide open.

Mudman was relentless. His fingers ran in and out of her at full speed while he sucked on her erect clitoris. Her juices leaked into his mouth, and he swallowed them almost hungrily. "Cum for me, shawty. Cum fo' daddy."

Keisha hated when he called himself her daddy. It sent shivers through her. She arched her back and screamed hard into his devouring mouth while a group of Latina women walked past the car and tried their best to look inside of the tinted windows.

Mudman sucked on her pussy lips one by one and smacked his lips. "Get yo' thick ass up hurr and ride me right now shawty. Hurry up." He let his seat back some more and pulled his piece out of his pants.

Keisha took ahold of it and licked her lips. She pumped it up and down in her small hand. It beat and felt incredibly hot. Another reason she loved Mudman so much was because he was packing a baby leg in his boxers. She stroked the monster and felt her pussy leaking.

"Go' 'head, suck dat, shawty. Fuck is you waiting on?" He wrapped his fingers into her hair and guided her on to his pole.

Keisha inhaled half of it and pulled her mouth back up. She licked around the head in a circular motion before swallowing the majority of him. She gagged and brought her mouth off of him. She looked into his eyes, then took the majority of him again before slurping like a pro. She came to her knees in the driver's seat, leaning all the way into his lap.

Mudman ran his hand over her booty. He dipped lower and found her pussy. He dipped two fingers inside of her while she handled her bidness. He shot them in and out of her in a blur. She was leaking in no time.

"Fuck, Keisha, get yo' ass up hurr right now and sit on dis dick. Come on."

Keisha straddled his lap, facing the windshield. She reached under herself and held him steady while she slid down on to him. As soon as he parted her lips, she came. Then she came again when she felt all of him inside of her.

Mudman pulled her all the way back and sucked on her neck. "Ride me like a killa. Make dis ma'fuckin' Hellcat rock. Come on, bitch."

"Uhh! Okay." She took ahold of the dashboard and began to fuck Mudman. She bounced back into his lap while he pulled her hard nipples and sucked on her neck loudly. The deeper he went, the more she came. She held her own lips open so she could watch his dick split her pink. This sight excited her.

Mudman held her titties. He bounced her up and down. He could feel her making his lap stickier. It felt good. When she screamed that she was cumming again, he could no longer hold back. He came skeeting into her over and over again.

Keisha continued to bounce up and down, milking him. When his last remnant entered into her womb, she fell back against him, breathing hard. He licked the sweat off of her neck and sucked on her earlobe. Neither of them paid any attention to the crowd of beachgoers that watched their sexcapade through the front windshield. The thrill of being watched only heightened their romp.

"Like I said, when I get home tonight, I'm fucking dat ass, you hear me, baby?" Mudman spat aggressively.

She nodded with his dick still lodged deep within her. "Yeah, bae, I hear you."

Chapter 3

Figgady pulled the 2020 cherry red Benz truck up to Mr. D's night lounge and stepped out with four of his gunmen behind him. Figgady dusted off his Burberry 'fit and turned his fitted cap all the way to the back. When he got to the back door of the club, he was met by a 6'6" bouncer that looked him up and down as if he already had a problem.

Figgady stepped up to him and looked him in the eye. "Say, mane, I got a meeting with Lucas."

The bodyguard looked him over closely. "Lucas told me that I was supposed to meet you right hurr in this here parking lot. He said when you got hurr that I was supposed to escort you inside. But just you. Guess he wanna talk some serious bidness."

Figgady nodded. "I already know dat. Sooner you get the fuck out of my way, the sooner I can make it to my meeting." Figgady looked back at his killas, and then forward into the eyes of the big bodyguard. "Watch out, nigga."

It was ninety degrees outside. Even at night, Baton Rouge was hot and humid. The mosquitoes were biting. This caused the locals to be automatically irritated. People seemed to walk around annoyed just because of the weather and bugs.

The bodyguard shook his head. "Say, mane, I don't give a fuck what you thought was supposed to be taking place, but the only person Lucas approved to be coming inside of his lounge tonight was you. You gon' have to leave the entourage outside. I'm sorry."

Figgady scoffed. "Oh really?"

The bodyguard nodded. "Yeah, really." He refused to back down just because Figgady was with a few other men. He felt that Lucas had given him specific orders. If he wanted to move up in the game, then he was going to follow them to the tee.

"Matter fact, they gotta leave off of the premises. If a could have been ain't doing bidness directly with the boss, den they gotta g-"

Instead of listening to what he had to say, Figgady had already looked back at his homies and given them the eye. Before the man could even finish his words, all four shooters had two pistols apiece cocked and aimed at him. The bodyguard threw his hands up and stopped talking. Figgady mugged him with intense hatred before he grabbed him by the throat and slammed his forehead to his. "Nigga, you just not know who da fuck I am, do you?"

The bodyguard began to tremble. Sweat dripped off of his dark-skinned face. "Say, mane, I was just doing what Lucas told me to do," he croaked because Figgady still had his neck gripped.

Figgady increased the pressure and added a second hand. He didn't give a fuck if it was out in the open. He demanded respect. He choked him as hard as he could. The bodyguard slapped at his hands.

"Nigga, I'm Figgady. I got the streets. Baton Rouge is mine. I go anywhere I wanna go. Fuck Lucas's orders, do you hear me?" He squeezed harder, and harder.

The bodyguard could feel the bones in his neck crushing. He could no longer breathe. He had a cold, and his nose had been stopped up since the morning. He folded backward and wound up on the ground. He felt like his heart was getting ready to burst. He saw that Figgady's Rounds continued to keep their weapons pointed down on him. He knew that there was nothing that he could do other than hope that Figgady released him before the life left his body.

Figgady knelt with one knee on the concrete of the parking lot, choking harder and harder. He shook and watched the man's eyes roll to the back of his head. Before he killed him, he slammed him to ground and stood up. The bodyguard rolled on the pavement, coughing. Figgady mugged him some more.

"Nigga, get yo' punk ass up and lead us to Lucas. If there are any more problems out of you, I'm gon' personally take you out the game." Figgady could already feel his blood boiling. His eyes were bucked wide open. He tasted murder in the air. Baton Rouge appeared to be calling for it.

The bodyguard jumped up and staggered around on his feet. He held his throat and waved for Figgady and his crew to follow him. When they got inside, he led them to the back of the lounge and up a row of stairs that took them to the second floor of the club. Once there, they traveled down a hallway until they were standing in front of Lucas's door. The bodyguard knocked on it and continued to hold his throat.

Lucas opened the door and frowned when he saw the number of men standing in the hallway. He was 5'8" tall, heavyset, and light-skinned. "Grant, what the fuck is all dis?" he questioned.

Figgady bumped past him and into the medium-sized office. He cleared everything off of Lucas's desk with one swipe of his arm. His laptop and phone crashed to the floor. Figgady glared at him. "Lucas, sit yo' bitch ass down, we need to talk."

Lucas slid his hand under his shirt and clutched the handle of his .45. Before he could bring it from under his shirt, Figgady's gunmen had him slammed against the wall with barrels being forced into his skull so hard that his skin torn and bled. It had happened so fast that he was caught off guard.

"Nigga, you betta drop that muthafuckin' gun and sit yo' ass down. We ain't playin' with you," Figgady said, almost bored. He pulled a half gram of tar out of his pocket and opened the packaging of aluminum foil. He made two lines and tooted both of them while Lucas was slammed into his chair across from him. His gun was yanked away aggressively.

Lucas was angry. "Man, why da fuck you coming at me like I'm a ho-ass nigga, Figgady? I accepted this meeting out of respect for you and yo' niggas. But you playing dis shit all wrong."

"Nigga, in two days you getting a shipment in of that ninety-eight percent pure shit. My sources tell me that it's gon' be about fifteen bricks. All Sinaloa," Figgady said, pulling on his nose. He felt the heroin coursing through his system. His eyelids got heavy. It was a volatile mix with the six ounces of pure codeine that he'd already consumed.

Lucas was taken aback. "How da fuck you know what I got going on?"

"Fifteen birds, nigga. I wanna take all eight off your hands, for ten apiece," Figgady said, sitting back in his seat and looking Lucas in the eye.

"Ten apiece, nigga, you out yo' muthafuckin' mind. I'm making every bit of thirty five thousand a key. What the fuck would make me give 'em to you for ten apiece?"

Boom! Boom! Boom! The gun jumped in Figgady's hand. Lucas's bodyguard fell face first on the table in from of him. Half of his face had been knocked away. He slowly slid off of the table and hit the floor. Figgady held the smoking gun. "Bitch-ass nigga, dat's why. I ain't asking yo' punk ass; I'm telling you."

Lucas watched Grant's body spill its contents on the floor of the office. He couldn't believe Figgady's moxie. He knew that he was in no position to negotiate with a loose cannon. He needed to survive to see another day. He could always get the upper hand at another time. First he would try another tactic. He nodded. "Look, mane, instead of you strong arming me for my lil shipment, say I put you on to some other cats that are using the same route I am, but they getting a whole lot more work. You thank we could work somethin out better than dat fifteen a key shit?"

"Nigga, I said ten a key." Figgady eyed him coldly. "My bad, you know what I meant." Lucas laughed nervously. "Say, mane, I'm talking thirty keys, all pure. Da same night I get my shit! You interested in dat?"

Figgady sat back in his chair. He looked across the table at Lucas. "Nigga, talk slow, and make some sense for me. If I detect any bullshit, on gang, you gon' wind up like dat fuck nigga down durr. Now talk," Figgady ordered.

***

Mudman pulled his mask over his head and wiggled his fingers into his black leather gloves. He'd latched the vest as tight as he could across his chest. He lowered himself in the passenger's seat of Payroll's van. He looked down Second Street and saw three dudes waking back and forth talking on their cell phones.

Payroll already had the Jason Voorhees mask over his face. He peeped his rivals through the binoculars and smiled under his mask. "You see, we having a turf war right now, Mudman. Before we lock down dis plug coming out of Mexico, we gotta clear dese niggas from off da deck. The more we kill dis week, the easier its gon' be to move in next week. Dis is Oakland, and it's just how dis shit go."

"Nigga, say no mo'. I don't give a fuck about dese niggas. I'm tryna get my hands on some of those pieces come up Interstate 5 next week. What you say dat shit like again?"

Payroll slammed a hunnit round clip into his Draco and cocked it on the side. "It's ninety-eight percent. We can step on dat shit three times, and it still a knock a nigga socks off.

Its good money, but before we can even think about getting our bag up, we gotta move these clowns around. Let's do this." He ducked low and crawled to the back of the van beside Mudman. Two members from his crew passed them and took the driver's seat, and the other took the passenger's seat.

Mudman rolled the side door to the van all the way open and sat back down. He had a hunnit round clip inside of his assault rifle and another in his side pocket. He was ready for war at all costs. This was the type of shit that made him get out of the bed in the morning. "Mane, step on dat gas, and let's give dese niggas hurr every thang they can stand," he said in his strong southern drawl.

Payroll liked Mudman already. Ever since he had come from Baton Rouge, he'd been on bidness since day one. Payroll guessed that he already had five bodies under his belt, and he'd only been in Oakland less than a year. "Let's get it."

The van screeched from the curb and made a hard left on to the block full of the Filbert Street Cartel Boys. They seemed oblivious to the killas rolling down on them - until the van slammed on its brakes. Errrrrrr-UH! Smoke emitted from the tires.

Both Mudman and Payroll hopped out of the side of the van door with five of their behind them. Mudman was the first to blow at the crowd of rivals. He held the Draco against his shoulders and squeezed the trigger. His assault rifle roared as he hopped down the crowd, catching them loafing. His bullets flew out of his gun in rapid fashion. They tore up backs and knocked thick chunks out of Filbert Cartel necks. Mudman watched them fall to the ground. Instead of him jumping over them and continuing to gun, he stopped over the squirming bodies and emptied load after load into them. The shook on the ground as his bullets knocked massive holes into their already-leaking flesh.

Not to be outdone, Payroll let his Draco ride. The fire from his gun was bright in the dark night. He craved murder. He chased his enemies and kept gunning, even when the Filbert Cartel began to shoot back at them from their gangways.

Mudman whaled backward letting his assault rifle ride. He sprayed every place that he thought the return fire could have been coming from. His Draco vibrated in his hands and clicked. He pulled the empty magazine out of it and slammed another inside. He cocked it and kept on busting like crazy, making his way back toward the van.

Payroll's Draco clicked and alerted him that it was empty. The return gunfire from the enemies became heavy. He found himself zigzagging as he ran back to the van. Right before he jumped inside of it, the window to the van shattered. He wound up on the floor, breathing heavily. "Pull off, nigga, pull off!"

Mudman jumped in the side door and scooted backward. He was still blowing at the rival shooters as the van scurt away from the curb. They heard a loud BOOM! The front windshield shattered inward. Mudman jumped backward and hit his head on the van's back seat. "What the fuck was dat?"

The driver to their van fell on the floor with his brains leaking out of his face. He was dead before he even realized he'd been shot. The shooter in the passenger seat bucked in the direction he thought the shot had come from five times with his .9. Then he slid over, and got behind the steering wheel, which was covered in blood and meat. He stepped on the gas and pulled off. Shots began to riddle the van, knocking it from right to left. A steady tink, tink, tink echoed in the night. Mudman stayed low to the ground, his heart pounding in his chest. He didn't know whether to call that shoot out a victory or a loss. They had killed at least six and lost one. He guessed if you looked at it that way, then they had been victorious. He had a lot to learn about Oakland. He missed Baton Rouge.

***

Later that night, Payroll and Mudman threw their fallen comrade's body over the bridge and into the ocean. It was a regular occurrence for Payroll. He'd lost more than thirty of his homies in the last six months. In Oakland, a street nigga was lucky to see the age of thirty. He was twenty-five and knew that his time was short. All he kept telling himself was that before he went, he wanted to leave behind a bag of money to his wife and daughter, and he wanted the respect of the streets.

Mudman watched the body fall all the way down before it created a big splash. He dusted his gloves together and looked over to Payroll. "So now what?"

"Now we hunt the ones in charge and slay they asses. We on the clock too. My plug said that before he put that work in my hands, he wanna know that it's going to be money being made, and not war. It is impossible to war and make bags of cash. A true street nigga gon' be dedicated to one or the other. Come on, let's get the fuck out of here."

Mudman watched the body sink to the bottom of the ocean. Then he looked out at the bright lights of the city. He felt a twinge of sickness. Baton Rouge, seemed to be calling him.

Chapter 4

When Mudman got back to the Acorn Projects that night, he felt tired and exhausted. He'd been up two days straight, with only minimal amounts of sleep, trapping with Payroll and trying his best to learn the slums of Oakland. He stepped into the apartment, and the first thing he smelled was Prada perfume. That brought a short smile to his face. He eased inside and locked the door behind him. He heard laughing. Now his smile was turned into a murderous mug. He pulled his .40 Glock off of his hip and crouched down. The apartment was pitch black, but he was a born hunter. He closed his eyes for a second and then opened them. They adjusted to the darkness right away. He navigated through the small living room and into the hallway. He heard murdered voices. He tried to detect a male's voice. He knew that Keisha wasn't stupid enough to fuck with him like that, but then again, he didn't trust nobody. He waited for a second and listened. There was silence all of a sudden. Mudman placed his ear on the bedroom door and sniffed the air. Once again, the scent of Prada spoke to him. He tried the knob and twisted it. Very slowly he eased it open, just enough for him to peer inside of the room.

There lay Keisha on the bed. She had on a tight skirt. It was raised up on her cheeks. Both chocolate globes were half exposed. In her crack was a red thong. She was without a blouse. All she wore was a matching red bra. Her titties threatened to spill out of them. He was able to see her from a side view. His eyes trailed from her on to the thick female laying on the side of her.

Mudman guessed that she was young, probably no older than eighteen. She was high yellow with curly black hair. She wore a pair of booty shorts that were all up in her ass crack.

She had her right thigh pulled upward. Mudman was able to see how her pussy was molded to her panties. He made out a hint of a red lip. When she spread her other leg, it really busted her gap wide open. He felt his dick getting hard and hoped that Keisha and the girl were about to get it in.

The girl reached over and rubbed Keisha's booty. She laughed. "I know yo' butt still hurt, you fell kind of hard there." She kept right on rubbing.

Keisha laid on her stomach and closed her eyes. "I still don't know how I fell. I just got dizzy as hell, and before I knew it, I was hitting the ground." She ran her tongue over her lips and moaned deep in her throat.

The girl squeezed her booty and smacked it a bit. She laughed and took her hand away. She stood up on her knees on the bed. "I'll be back. I gotta use the bathroom." She hopped out of the bed with her nipples rock hard on her DD breasts. Mudman saw the mold of her cat against her shorts again, and his piece jumped up and down. She looked so thick and fine to him. He wondered who she was. He slid into the hallway and back into the living room. He peeked around the corner. He watched the girl close the door to their bedroom. She took a deep breath with her back to it. Then she slid her hand into her panties and rubbed her pussy. She walked into the bathroom and closed the door. Mudman closed the distance quick. He rested his ear on the wood, and after only a minute, he could hear her moaning. Now he was really wondering who she was.

He opened the door to his bedroom real slowly and caught Keisha tweaking her already-hard nipples through her bra, with her eyes closed. She moaned and opened her thick thighs wide. She rubbed the cloth between her legs until a wet spot appeared on the front.

"Keisha," Mudman whispered.

She opened her eyes. When she was able to fully focus in on his image, her eyes bucked wide open and she sat up. Her thick nipples were like eraser tips. "Baby, when did you get in?" She slid out of the bed and walked over to him.

Mudman pulled her to him and gripped that ass. She moaned and leaned her face into his neck. "I just got in. Who is li'l shawty that was just in hurr rubbing all over yo' ass and shit?" he questioned, feeling his dick press against her. He clutched her ass cheeks more roughly.

Keisha stepped forward to feel it better. His male hardness began to drive her crazy. "Boy, you talking about Savanna?"

Mudman sucked her neck. "I don't know shawty name. She was just in hurr though." He slid his hand into her panties from the back and dipped two fingers into her pussy.

She moaned. "Mmm. Dat's Sandra's li'l daughter. You know, Payroll's baby mother. She ain't nothing but seventeen. Dat girl love me though. We was just chilling, dat's all."

Mudman could feel that her pussy was soaking wet. It dripped off of his wrist. "Dat lip bitch was all over yo' ass. Den she went in the hallway to rub her lil gap. You got her feeling some type of way." He ran his fingers in and out of her at moderate speed.

Keisha humped backward into his digits. She was groaning deep within her throat. "Don't say dat, Mudman, she just a baby."

Mudman slung her over the bed and kicked her feet apart. He pulled out his dick and ran it up and down her slit. She was dripping like crazy. He slid in and held her ass cheeks in his lap. "Dat bitch got yo' pussy wet, don't she? You liked letting her rub all on this big ass, huh?"

Keisha shivered. "Please don't do this, baby. She gon' catch us." Keisha felt his dick throb in her tight pocket. She emitted a moan when he pulled out and slammed back forward as hard as he could. Then he took ahold of her hips and got to fucking her like an animal.

"Tell me dat lip bitch turned you on. Tell me," he ordered, long stroking her.

Keisha growled. She slammed back into his lap over and over. "Uhhhh! Rome!" She laid her face on the bed while he fucked her as only he could. Her panties were all up the crack of her ass.

Mudman sucked his middle finger and slid it into her back door. He wanted to open that ass right up. He was feening for some of it. "Tell me, Keisha."

"No. No. No. No. She just…uh… She just a…li'l girl. Uhhhh! Fuck!" She felt Mudman dip two fingers into her rose bud and came hard.

Savanna pulled her fingers out of her box and perked up. She could have sworn that she heard Keisha moaning. She wondered if the rubbing of her ass had affected her in the same way that it had done her. She stood up and sucked her fingers clean. Then she opened the bathroom door and stuck her head out. Sure enough, Keisha's moans were louder. Savanna's nipples began to hurt. She hurried to the bedroom door and saw that it was opened just a crack. She peered inside and immediately slid her hand back into her panties. Her fingers found her opening and slid inside.

Mudman was fucking Keisha at full speed and jabbing her ass at the same time with his fingers. He felt his cum building inside of him. He pulled out his piece and came all over her chocolate ass cheeks. She reached back and rubbed it into her skin.

Mudman knocked her hand away. "I told you I wanted some of dis ass, didn't I?" He positioned himself. The Percocets and pink Mollie had him hard as a rock, and feening for some of her ass. He slid in and immediately got to working her bowels.

Savanna squatted in the doorway, fingering herself like crazy at the sight before her. She'd watched Mudman pull what looked like a long, brown, shiny cucumber from out of Keisha with a sucking noise before he lined himself back up and slid it into her ass. It was almost too much for her to handle.

Keisha beat on the bed as she rocked back into him at full speed. "Rome! Rome! Rome! Uhh, fuck me! I love you! I love you so much!" she screamed, not caring if Savanna heard them. She was oblivious to the fact that they were being watched. She growled and reached under her belly. She took ahold of her clit and pinched it hard. This sent a strong shudder through her before she came.

Mudman felt her gripping him. He pushed her forward, and fell on top of her, fucking her ass with all he had. Fifty hard pumps later, he came deep inside of her bowels, smacking that ass, squeezing it like Savanna had done. He left himself implanted for a few minutes, then he rolled off of her. He fell on his side and locked eyes with Savanna. She was squatted down with her back against the wall, working herself over. When they locked eyes, she stopped and jumped up. She rushed into the hallway and back into the bathroom, embarrassed.

Mudman closed his eyes and was asleep in a matter of minutes.

***

Figgady pulled the belt from around his arm and injected the Sinaloa into his system. The tar mainlined directly to his heart. His eyes rolled into the back of his head. He licked his dry lips and sighed. He felt light, and then numb all over.

Prentice sat across the table from him. He slammed the thousand dollar stack of money in front of Figgady. "Mane, tell me whurr da fuck dat nigga and dat bitch at right now? You s'posed to have loyalty to me, and not they snake asses." Prentice held his ribs and adjusted himself in the chair.

Behind him stood two of his Reapers. They were young, cold-hearted savages with lost souls that he kept hopped up on heroin and pills. They were from the projects of Baton Rouge and doted on his every word. They were silently hoping that Prentice gave them the word to take Figgady out. Figgady and his crew of Animals were terrorizing Baton Rouge. They had the city shook. There was a fifty thousand dollar bounty on Figgady's head placed by the Dominicans out of Lawrence in Boston. Word had gotten back to Baton Rouge about the kick down that Figgady and his crew had pulled. Now the money was on his head and up for grabs.

Figgady pulled his nose. "Mane, every time I see yo' ass you ask me the same shit. I done told your homeboy that I don't get down like dat durr. That rat shit is for mice, not real niggas like fat folk. Nigga, you wanna find bruh n'em, you gon' have to do dat work yo'self. Now the reason I called dis meeting is 'cause we finna lock down the south. Every muthafucka dat's over dere hustling finna be fish food, boy. Mark my words on dat right dere."

Prentice mugged him. They were sitting in his basement with a red light bulb screwed in. Prentice kept a black bandana across half of his face, and so did his killas. They were Reapers. Pure killas. Prentice was head of their crew, and his heart was black as dirt in the cemetery after how Keisha and Mudman had betrayed him. He leaned forward and crossed his fingers. "Before we get on dat shit durr, let me show you something." He stood up and pulled off his shirt. He ran his fingers over the bullet wounds that both Keisha and Mudman had given him. "You see dis shit right hurr? Dem ma'fuckas tried to take me out of the game. They shot me more times than I can count. I still got bullets all up in me. The doctors say if they moved three specific ones that I would be paralyzed for the rest of my life. They also said that if a ma'fucka was to tackle me the wrong way that it could kill me. How da fuck you think dat make me feel?"

Figgady eyed him from across the table. "Nigga, all dat shit ain't got nothin' to do wit' me. I called dis meeting because I'm letting you know what I'm finna do to dis south before I take my vacation. If you got any niggas over durr that you care about, you betta let dem niggas know what it is right now. Ma'fuckas got three days to move around. If they ain't gone or relocated in dat amount of time, den its dey fault. But I'm letting you know right now, we cleaning dat bitch out. All spoils go to the Cutthroats. I'm standing on dat." He leaned back in his chair and ran his tongue over his gold teeth.

Prentice felt his heart pounding in his chest. He imagined himself blowing Figgady's face off. He eyed him evilly from across the table. "Nigga, I don't give a fuck about shit you finna do to dem boys out South, as long as you let me know where I should be looking for Mudman and dis bitch. You let me do my thang, and whatever you Cutthroats do is y'all bidness. Us Reapers won't intervene. You got my word on dat."

Figgady mugged Prentice for a long time. He nodded his head and laughed. The spot where he injected his Tar began to itch. He scratched the injection site. "Nigga you must got me fucked up. I wasn't telling you because I was looking for your permission. I was telling you because dis shit gon' happen whether you want it to or not. If you had a few potnas out dat way trapping, it's best to tell dem to move around or dey finna be casualties of war. We on no mercy shit right now. Ya feel me?"

Prentice watched him scratch himself. He took the pistol in his waistband and adjusted it. Every fiber of his being was telling him to unload on Figgady. He didn't like the youngster and felt that Figgady's head was getting too big. "Say, mane, if I had some potnas out dat way, you n'em Cutthroat Boys wouldn't be doing shit. Lucky for you I don't. So, I guess what I'm saying is, do what you do, but keep all dat shit thurr across dem tracks, and remember who running da rest of Baton Rouge."

Figgady laughed. He slammed both of his hands on the table and stood up. The sudden noise had caught Prentice off guard. It pissed him off.

"Let me tell you somethin' right now. Don't a muthafucka breathing call shots over the Cutthroats. The only reason you being hip to what I'm finna do is because I respect you. I don't fear you, nigga. Just respect you. Let me make dat shit perfectly clear." He stared into his eyes, feeling murderous. He imagined melting Prentice's face with a blow torch. He cackled. "Cutthroats, we up out dis bitch."

Prentice remained silent while he watched Figgady and his crew leave from his basement as if they had just stood on him. He nodded his head.

"A'ight den, dat's how we finna play shit? Cool." He slapped his hand on the table in anger. Then he stood up and flipped it over before his old bullets wounds reminded him that he wasn't as healthy as he thought. The pain took his breath away. He fell to his knees and gritted his teeth. He had to find Mudman and Keisha. He would do whatever it took to get his revenge on the pair. If Figgady wanted to test this fact, then he was sure to soon find out, Prentice promised himself.

Chapter 5

It was three o'clock in the morning. Hot and humid. The rain had stopped only a half hour prior. Payroll looked both ways before creeping into the backyard of Cartier with Mudman following close behind him. When it came to the Filbert Cartel Boys, Cartier was the second in command of the dope boys. The first head, Nike, was doing a short bit in the county jail, and was set to be released in three months. Payroll figured that it was best to handle Cartier while Nike was still away. He'd gotten some inside information from one of the Project Goddesses by the name of Tori. Tori had lived inside of the Acorn Projects since she was a newborn. Now at sixteen years old, she pledged her loyalties to her hood. It just so happened that Cartier had a weakness for Tori. He was obsessed with her fuck game, a fuck game that Payroll had trained her in.

Mudman held the five shot automatic shotgun up against his shoulder. He looked across the backyard and back to the alley from whence they had come. Three of Payroll's henchmen rested with their back against the two story house. All were armed and ready to spill some blood. Mudman looked back over at Payroll. He gave him the nod.

Payroll scratched at the back door as if he was a cat or dog. He stood back and waited. The signal was already discussed in advance by him and Tori.

A minute later, Tori opened the door and stepped into the night. She saw how deep Payroll and his killas were, and suddenly felt a wave of remorse for Cartier. She swallowed her spit and stepped in front of Payroll. She grabbed his arm and pulled him away from the others. "Payroll, I don't think you should do this tonight. It's like ten people in there, and three of them are my girlfriends. You should do this another day."

Payroll couldn't believe what he was hearing. "What?"

Tori looked over his shoulder back toward the house. When she'd left from inside of it, Cartier and her friend Samantha were just headed into the bedroom where they were set to have sex for the very first time. Samantha was getting her initiation into their Filbert crew. Tori didn't want to ruin this. She and Samantha had been good friends for six years. "Tomorrow, Cartier will be there by his self. You should come holler at him then. If you do it now, you're going to be killing too many innocent people. You don't wanna do that, do you?"

Payroll grew instantly irritated. He didn't know what to say to Tori. To him, it sounded like she was trying to back out for whatever reason. "How many people did you say was in there?"

"Like ten," she whispered.

"And what is everybody doing?" Payroll questioned.

"Cartier and Samantha are getting ready to do their thing. Some of Cartier's guys are breaking down some Tar in the kitchen, getting it ready for the streets, and a few of them are mingling with my girls in the living room. Tonight, is just not the best night. It wouldn't be smart. There are people in there that I care about."

Mudman mugged Payroll from across the yard. He had never been on a lick where there was this much talking prior too. He became upset, about to make his way over to Payroll, when Payroll upped his silenced .9 millimeter, slammed it to Tori's forehead, and pulled the trigger twice. Her face caved in before blood and brain shot out of her skull and dripped down her neck. She lay on the grass unmoving, but not dead. Payroll stood over her. He aimed and fired three more face shots. Then he faced Mudman. "Let's go."

Mudman was the first one into the house. He rushed up the back steps and into the backdoor. The open door led to a kitchen. Right there sitting at the kitchen table were three of Cartier's men. They were busy bagging up Tar and listening to Nipsey Hussle, nodding their heads. Mudman stopped in the middle of the kitchen and aimed at the back of the head closest to him. He pulled the trigger. Boom! He watched the man's head burst. His body fell to the floor, shaking. Then Mudman was finger-fucking his shotgun.

Payroll ran into the house and left Mudman in the kitchen shooting. He rushed up the stairs that led to Cartier's bedroom. He didn't waste any time. He figured that Cartier had heard the shots and was going for his gun. Payroll kicked the door open as hard as he could and got to spraying his Uzi.

Cartier held Samantha around the neck in front of him. Four of Payroll's bullets hit her up. Cartier fired his Glock back at Payroll. Boom! Boom! Boom! Boom! He knocked massive chunks out of the wall.

Payroll jumped back into the hallway. "Bitch-ass nigga! Acorn in dis bitch!"

Cartier busted back. He jumped out of the open window. He fell two stories down and snapped his ankle. "Uh!" he hollered, rolling around on the ground.

Payroll ran to the window and got to bucking down at him.

Cartier stood up and busted twice. He hopped along the side of the house. He needed to get to his truck parked in the back. He would get Payroll's bitch ass, he swore. He should have killed him a long time ago, he thought. He hobbled and ran as fast as he could.

Payroll jumped out of the back window, and on to the balcony. He had his Uzi tucked into the small of his back. He jumped down and cocked it. As soon as he got ready to meet Cartier halfway, Cartier caught him slipping. He ran at Payroll busting. *Boom! Boom! Boom! Boom! Boom!* The lights flashed over and over in the night.

Payroll was hit by the first three bullets. He flew backward and tried to shoot back. His slugs wound up flying aimlessly into the air before he hit the ground. It felt like lava holes were being seared into his stomach and chest. He struggled to breathe. Cartier hopped over to him with a big smile on his face.

"Hell yeah, Cuz!" He aimed his gun down at Payroll. "Nigga, I finally got yo' punk ass. Say yo' prayers." He bit into his lower lip and placed his finger around the trigger.

Bocka!

Cartier felt the bullet rip through the back of his head. He watched his brains leak all over his nose before he fell on his knees. Keisha rushed over and kicked him in the back. She stood over him and emptied her clip. She left her gun smoking. "Fuck nigga, get up off my cousin."

Mudman ran into the backyard to assess the damage. He saw the state of Payroll, and his eyes got big. "Damn, bruh, what the fuck happened?"

Payroll couldn't talk. He gritted his teeth and took deep breaths. He reached out for Keisha. He groaned as blood came out of the corners of his mouth. "Help me."

Mudman ran into the alley. He pulled the van as close to the backyard as possible. Then he ran and scooped up Payroll with the help of three of Payroll's guys. They got him into the van and hurried off to the hospital.

***

Figgady was sitting on the couch counting fifty thousand dollars in cash by hand when Chela, his baby mother, walked into the room with a blue silk Victoria's Secret robe wide open. Underneath, she wore the matching see through panties and no bra. Chela stood in front of him.

"Papi, you been in here counting money all night. Are you ever gon' come back here so you can tend to me?"

Figgady was fucked up. He'd just shot up a gram of ninety percent pure heroin, and that was after he popped two Percocet sixties. "Mane, I gotta count dis hurr paper. Dat pussy can wait. I'll be back durr to fuck wit' you in a minute."

Chela felt offended. She wanted to fuck. They hadn't gotten down in nearly a month. She was starting to think that there was something wrong with her that he didn't like. Once upon a time, he couldn't get enough of her Dominican pussy. "Count dat shit later, papi, I wanna fuck, come on."

Figgady looked up at her. He was feeling real violent because of the misunderstanding he'd had with Prentice. Second to that, he hated when any female disobeyed his orders. He didn't give a fuck who she was. "Shawty, check dis shit out. You already know how I get down. Now it's muthafuckin, money over bitches. That's all bitches, even my baby mama. Now take yo' ass back dere and wait on a nigga. I'll be back dere in a minute."

Chela smacked her lips. "A'ight, well fuck you den. I don't need to keep sweating you. You must have forgot that you dealing with a bad bitch?" She ran her fingers through her hair and fluffed it out down her back. "A million niggas out there that would die to get some of dis pussy." She turned her back on him and made her way down the expanse of the hallway.

Figgady jumped from the couch so fast that he left money all over the floor and table. He grabbed Chela by the hair and yanked her backward, slinging her to the floor. "And bitch, you must have forgot that you dealing with a killa?" He dragged her down the hallway by her long hair and let her go outside of the guest bedroom.

Chela hopped up and made a run for the front door. "Leave me alone, papi. I'm sorry. Please." She struggled to get the door open.

Figgady pulled his Ferragamo belt from around his waist and chased her into the front room. He swung the belt and whacked her across the back with it hard. "Bitch, let dat door go!" he hollered.

Chela continued to try and turn the lock. She did it successfully and was about to open the door when Figgady grabbed a handful of her hair again. He tossed her to the floor. She scooted backward om her ass. "Okay, papi, okay. I'ma leave you da fuck alone. I promise."

Figgady was already mad. He raised the belt and brought it down over and over again. "You. Always. Running. Yo'. Muthafuckin'. Mouth!" He whooped harder and harder.

Chela tried her best to block his assaults. She bounced off of the floor and rushed him, swinging with her eyes closed like a mad woman. Her fists whipped through the air, and one of them caught him on the bottom of his chin. He dropped to the floor, briefly unconscious. The pills and Tar had made him weaker than normal. Chela kept swinging at the air, not knowing that Figgady was knocked out cold. By the time she figured it out, she was out of breath and musty.

She looked down and saw that Figgady lay on his side, dropped. She couldn't believe her eyes. She knelt down and rested her hand on his shoulder. She could hear him snoring. "Baby? Baby? Wake up." she ordered.

Figgady was in another world. He couldn't hear her, nor could he hear anything else. He was out of there. He grunted and began to snore harder.

Chela panicked. She knew that when he finally did wake up and found out that she had knocked him out, he was going to kill her. She became depressed. "Fuck man."

Her daughter, Chiah, came out of the bedroom with tears in her eyes. "Mama, are y'all done fighting?" she whimpered.

Chela rushed over to her and grabbed her hand. "Baby, we gotta get out of here. Come on." She pulled her along while she grabbed her car keys. She could still feel the shape from where Figgady had assaulted her.

"But where we finna go? We can't leave Daddy like dis?" Chiah said.

Chela wasn't trying to hear her six-year-old daughter. She grabbed her around the wrist and pulled her from the house, after placing a jacket around her shoulders. As soon as they got on to the porch, she called the only person she knew would help them and be able to calm Figgady down when he did wake up. She called his big homie, Prentice.

Chapter 6

It was two months later. After Payroll had been admitted into the hospital and cared for, Twelve had rushed in and handcuffed him to the bed. He was later detained for three outstanding warrants and bail jumping. A month later they would also charge him with the murder of Cartier. Mudman assumed an alias and went to see him in the county jail. He felt uncomfortable as he settled into the small booth. He picked up the phone and wiped it down as best he could with a wet wipe. Being in that atmosphere brought back all kinds of bad memories to him from when he was in Angola.

Payroll limped to the phone and visiting booth. He sat with his colostomy bag on the side of him. Cartier's bullets had ripped a major portion of his small intestine away from him. He groaned, closed his eyes, and picked up the phone. "What it do, Cuz?"

Mudman wasn't with all that "Cuz" shit. He was from Baton Rouge, and back there, his killas didn't roll with the same things that other cities did. They set clicked and went from there. "What's it looking like?"

Payroll exhaled and shook his head. "They trying to pin Cartier's murder on me. They say that night that supposedly me and Loc was supposed to have a shootout. They found gunshot residue on my hands, and slugs in him from my gun, of course. I know I can beat all this other shit, but that murder right there looking like its gon' be a task."

Mudman shook his head. He scanned his surroundings, and made sure that no enemies were present, before he turned back to Payroll. "So, what you need from me?"

"Lawyer money. I'm talking at least two hunnit G's. I want the best lawyer that money can buy. In order for me to get that, I gotta spend that bag."

"How much cake you got put up?" Mudman asked. He was thinking that two hundred thousand dollars news was a li'l steep, and besides, he didn't even know Payroll like that. He silently didn't give a fuck what his outcome would be.

"About twenty racks, but Sandra gon' need that to get by until I can figure dis shit out. I was really banking on plugging in with them Sinaloa 46 fuckas. That's millions right there, Mudman, believe me when I tell you dis."

"Well, ain't no sense in wishful thanking now, that shit dead. We gotta move forward. Its gon' be ugly trying to come up with that bread out here with no plug. Two hunnit steep, but I'ma see what I can do."

Payroll lowered his eyes. "I ain't ask for Keisha's help. She grabbed my burner from my closet and helped me. Nigga, I'd rather be resting in Black Heaven than to be in this predicament.

Mudman glared at him. He couldn't believe that he'd just said all of that dumb shit over the phone. Yeah, it was true that Keisha had used his gun to finish Cartier. Yeah, he didn't ask her to assist him, and yes, it was also true that had she not intervened when she did, that Cartier would have wound up killing him. "Say, mane, you talking stupid, li'l one. Just let me and my shawty bust a few moves. We gon' get as close to that two hunnit G's as we can."

"Justin Bivens. He wants fifty G's as a retainer. Do you at least got that tucked?"

"What?" Now Mudman was really getting offended because he felt like Payroll was trying to check his bag. He wasn't having that shit.

"Nall, I was just thinking that once I got a good lawyer, that he could argue for me to make bail. Justin Bivens is a beast when it comes to murder charges. He was trained by

Johnny Cochran's firm before he branched off and did his own thing. You get me him, and we good."

Mudman lowered his eyes and looked into those of Payroll. "What da fuck you saying, potna? You making it seem like you got some other shit on yo' mind."

Payroll clenched his jaw. "Nigga, I said what the fuck I said. Get me Justin Bivens. We all locked into this shit like cellies." Payroll stood up. "My niggas already got the word to fall under you. They gon' do whatever you say until I'm freed from dis. You got two weeks to get that first fifty G's. Grind how you grind. Do you. Just remember that I'm in need, and your loyalty depends on how this shit turns out for Keisha."

Mudman punched the glass and threw the phone against the bulletproof glass. He was heated. His chest moved up and down as if he was struggling to breathe. He wanted to kill Payroll. No nigga had ever been able to threaten his woman and get away with it. Mudman felt like niggas like Payroll deserved to be in the morgue.

Payroll laughed and walked away from the phone. He didn't give a fuck about Keisha. He didn't give a fuck about Mudman. He didn't give a fuck about nobody other than himself. If Mudman didn't come up with the cash in a swift enough fashion. he was going to spill the beans. He would deal with the consequences of ratting at another time. Right now, his freedom was most important. Nothing was more important to him than that.

***

That night, Mudman picked Keisha up and took her to the county fair. After the fair concluded, they wound up dining at a restaurant called Yoshi's Oakland. Keisha sat across from him, eating like a real woman. She made it halfway through her meal before she realized that Mudman had only picked over his. "Baby, what's the matter?" she asked, reaching across the table and touching his big hands.

Mudman eased back in his seat. He could feel the handles of his twin Glocks sticking him in his waistband. "I might have to murder Payroll."

Keisha damn near choked on her food. She grabbed a napkin and spit her chicken into it. "What? Why would you have to do that?"

"Because it turns out that homeboy ain't nothing but a bitch-ass nigga, dat's why." Mudman pulled out a knot of hundreds and dropped one on the table. "Come on, let's get the fuck up out of hurr."

"But I ain't had dessert yet."

"Keisha, fuck dat dessert. Get yo' ass up, and let's go. Talking 'bout some damn dessert," he snapped.

Keisha stood up and slammed the teddy bear that he had won her at the fair on top of the table. It landed in the remainder of the food. "Fine! But you ain't gotta be hollering at me Rome! Calm yo' ass down," she warned.

Mudman wanted to reach across the table and grab her by the neck. He looked over the restaurant. He saw that all eyes were on them. Both the white, and black customers' focus was pinned on them. "Let's go."

They made it outside and to the truck. Keisha tried her handle, but it was locked. She jiggled it impatiently. "Hurry the fuck up, Mudman. You rushing me and shit, now you slow poking. Hurry yo' ass up."

Mudman hit the locks from his remote. He kept calm as Keisha crossed her arms and waited outside of the truck in front of her passenger's door. "Fuck you waiting on? Get yo' ass in."

Keisha stomped her foot and crossed her arms with her Prada jacket in her hands. "Uh uh, you betta get yo' ass over hurr and open my ma'fuckin' door. Just cuz we over hurr in Oakland don't mean dat your southern manners didn't travel over hurr wit' you."

Mudman stopped in his tracks. He eyed her and flared his nostrils. Even though he was mad, he loved her, and as her man, he knew that it was his job to open all doors for her. That's how he was raised. He came around and opened the door for her. "Here, shawty."

Keisha smiled victoriously. "Thank you." She climbed into the truck and slammed the door.

Mudman got in on the other side. He started the engine and locked the doors. Before he could pull out of the parking lot, he grabbed Keisha by the throat and squeezed, choking her. He did this for ten seconds, and then slung her to the passenger's door. "Bitch, you betta never disrespect a muthafuckin' boss in public again. Fuck is you thanking? When I say let's go, you brang yo' ass," he roared. Had she been anybody else, he would have fucked her up.

Keisha bounced from the door and jumped on him. She wrapped her small hands around his neck and tried to choke the living daylights out of him. "How do this feel, huh? You thank just because you my old man that you can put yo' fuckin' hands on me?" she screamed.

Mudman slung her back into the passenger's seat. "Bitch, stay yo' ass right durr. If you cross dis ma'fuckin' console again, on Baton Rouge, I'm treating you like a nigga," he threatened.

"See, dat's dat bullshit right thurr, Mudman. You always gotta have da last word or get da last lick. Dat shit ain't cool." Keisha crossed her arm and sat back in the big leather seats.

Mudman pulled out of the parking lot. "Fuck what you talking 'bout. You my bitch. You do what the fuck I say. We in dese streets together, and I ain't kicked yo' ass to the curb yet. Dat should tell you every muthafuckin' thang you need to know. Long as I'm making shit happen for us, you gon' do what the fuck I say, and respect dis nigga right hurr."

"Yet? Did you just say you ain't kicked me to the curb yet? Really?"

"If you heard what the fuck I said, den ain't no need in me repeating myself."

Keisha nodded her head. "Okay, Mudman, you got that. Guess I should become one of dem submissive bitches, huh? Just let you treat me however you wanna treat me 'cause you making shit happen. Yeah, you'd love dat shit, wouldn't you?"

Mudman laughed. "Bitch, you muthafuckin right."

When they got home, Mudman held the door open for Keisha. She stormed into the apartment and slammed her coat down on the ground. She hurried to the back room and grabbed Mudman's Draco. She slammed a clip into it and cocked it. Then she was running back into the living room.

"Bitch-ass nigga, you wanna leave me? Huh? You been thinking about leaving me later on? Nigga, I'll kill yo' punk ass in cold blood. Dat's on my sister!" she screamed.

Mudman faced her and instantly his dick got hard. "Aw, bitch, you done iced a few niggas, now you thank you ready to kill me, huh? Dat what you thank?"

Keisha ran up on him and grabbed him by the throat. "I'll blow yo' shit all over dis living room if you ever thank you gon' leave me. Nigga, I love yo' ass to death. I'll take you out, and den me," she swore.

Mudman grabbed the barrel of the Draco and pressed it to his forehead. "Pull dat ma'fuckin' trigger. Murder me, bitch. You ain't got that Mudman shit in you yet. You faking." He grabbed her by the ass and squeezed it hard. He pressed his dick into her skirt's crease.

Keisha pressed the barrel harder into his forehead. She saw a trickle of blood. It excited her. She pressed it harder until the steel broke the skin even more. "I'll kill you, Mudman."

Mudman knocked her to the floor. She held on firm to the Draco. He ripped her panties from between her legs in one yank and slid into her hotness. He wasted no time before he was fucking her at full speed. "Kill me, Keisha! Kill Me! Kill me, bitch!"

Keisha wrapped her thighs around him and groaned deep within her throat. His dicking felt better and better. She grabbed the Draco and held to his neck. "Say only me. Unnnn. Unnnn. Unnnn."

Mudman grabbed her thigh and placed it on his shoulders. He got to digging her out. "You. My. Bitch. Keisha." Harder. Faster. He dug deeper, killing that pussy.

"Tell me." She placed her finger around the trigger. She would kill Mudman if he didn't confirm and it would only be her until the day they died. "Tell me!"

Mudman dug deeper. He couldn't deny how much he loved Keisha. She was his everything. The love of his life. She drove him crazy. Since day one, she always had.

Keisha felt an orgasm shattering through her. She closed her eyes as they rolled to the back of her head. "Say it. I'm your baby. Tell me just me! Please!"

Mudman huffed and puffed, fucking with all of his might. He felt the barrel on his neck, and imagined Keisha blowing his head off, and then herself. This made him cum as hard as he ever had before. He growled and nutted in her pussy again and again. Then he fell on top of her. "Just you, Keisha. You da only one that owns dis black heart. Dat's on Baton Rouge."

Keisha came at her those words. She wrapped her thighs around him and began kissing all over his lips.

***

Three hours later, they sat on the hood of Mudman's truck in the middle of the cemetery. Thirty feet in front of them lay three open graves where bodies had been lowered inside of caskets earlier that day. The cemetery was a calming place to be for Mudman. It kept him in touch with the reality that they all had to go sometime. He pulled Keisha closer to him and kissed the side of her forehead. "I love you, boo."

"I love you too, bae." The cemetery made Keisha think about her sister Kayla, who had passed away a little more than a year prior. "Baby, why do you thank you gotta do my cousin Payroll?"

Mudman kissed her forehead again. "Dat fuck nigga making it seem like he ready to drop a dime on you of I don't get him a lawyer."

"What?" Keisha looked Mudman over like he had lost his mind. She jumped off the hood of the car and stared at him.

Mudman slid off it. "Yeah, he said that shit when I went to see him earlier today."

Keisha was shocked. "You mean he actually said that he was gon' snitch on me of you don't get him an attorney?"

"Yeah, bitch, why the fuck you acting like it's so farfetched? Seems like you should know how that nigga get down seeing as he talking 'bout doing some fuck shit like dat anyway. "

"Don't be popping off at me. I'm just trying to find out what is going on." She hugged herself. She had a habit of doing that when she became nervous or worried about something. "So how would you handle his ass den? I already know you ain't 'bout to let no nigga get down on me like dat." "You already know dat." Mudman snatched her to him and brought his forehead to hers. "Don't play wit' me. You ain't gon' do shit but find out that I ain't like da rest of dese niggas out hurr. I love you to death. Ya understand dat right thurr?"

Keisha's pussy was wetter than Hurricane Katrina. "I love you, daddy. Dis shit hurr is forever until it ain't. Bury me next to my King when it's my time to go. Dat's on Baton Rouge." She pulled his head down and tongued him like she never had before. The entire time, all she could think about was the fact that Payroll was dead set on giving her up if Mudman didn't do what he said. She thought he was a punk, a rat, and lower than scum. She hoped against hope that she would be the one to take him out of the game. "I'm down for whatever, bae, you know dat."

Mudman gripped her ass. "Let me twerk his niggas first to run our bag up. Den I'ma do what I gotta do. A'ight?" He picked her up and sat her on the hood of the car. "I always wanted to taste dis pussy in the cemetery."

Keisha yanked up her skirt. "Nigga, you ain't said nothing but a word."

Chapter 7

Chela slid out of the bed and stretched with her arms over her head. The sun was shining brightly through the window. She could hear the birds chirping, and for some reason, it brought a smile to her face. She yawned and stretched as far to the ceiling as her fists would go, then covered her mouth. The short nightgown raised on her thick ass cheeks. She felt a draft and pulled it down.

Prentice peeped her from the doorway. He clutched his dick through his Polo shorts in one hand and her tray of food in the other. "Damn, shawty, you know you get finer and finer every day," he complimented her.

Chela blushed. She didn't know how to act around Prentice. She knew that he was Figgady's guy, and that both of them were killas. Sometimes she thought that when he flirted with her, he was just trying to test her to see what she would do. She always was extremely careful about how she responded.

Prentice came further into the room. "You didn't hear what I said, mami?"

Chela nodded. Now she was shy. Prentice was attractive to her. She tried her best not to let on that she visually desired him. "Yeah, I heard you. But what you expecting me to say?"

Prentice liked that jazzy shit. He liked that she appeared to not be afraid of him. That piqued his interest. He stepped in front of her. "You can say thank you. Dat's all I'm looking for." He held open his arms.

She looked him up and down before walking into them. She hugged him. She could feel all of his muscles. That, and the pole between his thighs. "Thank you, Prentice." She tried to release the hug.

Prentice held her tighter and ran his hands down her silk nightgown. They flirted over the expanse of her juicy ass. He wanted to squeeze the globes so bad but refrained. He backed up. "So, what's on yo' agenda for today?"

She walked back toward the bed. Her cheeks jiggled with each step. The scent of her was heavy in the room. Chela was a golden-colored Dominican. She was 5'3" tall. She weighed a hundred and thirty pounds even and had the body of a goddess. Her English was broken. To Prentice, and most men, she sounded so sexy.

"Don't know. I was thanking of giving Figgady a call. We need to work dis thang out. Plus, I miss him." She imagined the dark-skinned face of her man and grew depressed. She wondered if he thought about her too, or if he was dead set on killing her for her knocking him out.

Prentice felt offended. He wasn't about to allow Chela to break bad and return to Figgady that easy. He still had yet to get some of the treasures between her thighs. She'd been laid up in his pad for a month rent free, and something had to shake. "Say, shawty, I just seen the homeboy yesterday, and he still heated 'bout dat situation that happened between y'all. He said that as soon as he catch yo' ass, he feeding you to the gators," he lied. He hadn't seen Figgady in almost a month. The last time they had seen each other, all they did was mug one another.

Chela trembled. She imagined Figgady picking her up and tossing her into the swamp-infested alligator waters. Baton Rouge was famous for them. "What would make him tell you somethin' like dat?"

"We was talking 'bout my old lady. You remember Keisha? I thank you met her a few times."

She nodded. "You talking 'bout that chocolate girl, right? The one with that body and thangs?"

Prentice felt a twinge of jealousy at remembering how stacked Keisha had been. She had been stacked like that ever since the eighth grade. Prentice had gotten into more than a few fights battling for her honor. "Yeah, dat's hurr. Anyway, I guess he said he seen shawty the other day. He asked me if I still fucked with her because she ain't say nothin' 'bout me, and when I told him I didn't, dat's when he said that he ain't fuck wit' you no mo'. He said that when he catch you, he gon' blow off yo' kneecaps, and toss yo' ass in the swamp as alligator food."

Chela lowered her head. "Damn, it don't even matter that I got his daughter or none of that?" She felt defeated. After all they had been through... She had even turned on her family for Figgady. How was it that he couldn't let go of one lucky punch, she wondered?

Prentice slid back in front of her. He held her small waist and looked into her hazel eyes. "Shawty, I ain't wit' dat shit durr. I ain't 'bout to let nothin' happen to you or dat baby in dere. As far as I'm concerned, you ain't got shit to worry about. You can just stay hurr for as long as you need too. It's all good." His hands slowly slid down until they were covering her ass.

Chela flinched. She tried to back up out of his embrace. "Thank you, Prentice. I really appreciate it. I'ma make some calls to see if I can get in touch with a family member or something. That way me and my daughter won't be in your space." She tried to ease away from him.

Prentice held on to her. "N'all, shawty, you ain't gotta do all dat. It's good. Besides, you already been staying hurr dis long. Might as well see dis shit through." He gripped her ass and cuffed the cheeks. It felt soft as a pillow, and hot as cornbread. His piece stretched immediately.

Chela place her hands on his shoulders and pushed him away from her. "What da fuck are you doing? Don't you know dat I am your guy's baby mother?" she questioned. She glared at him angrily. "It's not cool, man."

Prentice flew in front of her and jacked her against the wall. He choked her with one hand and slid the other between her thighs. He rubbed her panty front. He could feel the warm, rubbery feeling of her sex lips. He leaned in and placed his lips to her ear. "Bitch, I don't know what the fuck you thank dis hurr is, but ain't shit free in dis world." He slid his hand from around her neck. They traveled further down to her C-cup breasts. He rubbed all over them and took the time out to pull on her nipples, which were poking through her gown.

Chela was shaking. She looked over his shoulder to her sleeping daughter. "Prentice, what are you saying right now?"

"Bitch, I'm saying you already know what dis is right now. You got all dis hurr pussy, and I want some of it." He sniffed along her throat and dipped his hand into her satin panties. His middle finger separated the folds of her sex.

Her clit was already engorged. Prior to her coming to stay with Prentice, Figgady had not touched her in weeks. She hated herself for feeling some type of way. She pushed against him. There was no way that she could cheat on her man. That foul shit wasn't in her. "Let me go, Prentice. We're not finna do dis hurr. Not against my man. Not while my daughter is in the room."

"What?" Prentice picked her up and held her against the wall by her ass. He sucked on her neck and stuffed his hand back into her panties. Once there, he found her opening. He slid two fingers into her and jammed them inside of her at rapid speed.

Chela closed her eyes. "Stop. Stop. Stop. Please. Aw. Aw. Shit. Ooooooh!" She bit into his shoulder and came watching her child squirm on the bed. She prayed that she didn't wake up.

Prentice added a third finger. Now his arm was going so fast that it started to hurt him. He lowered her to the carpet and laid on his side while he continued to finger her for all she was worth. "Cum again, bitch! Cum for me!" He lowered his face to her box, pulled her panties to the side, and sucked hard on her clit. His fingers continued to go crazy.

Chela arched her back. She bit into the back of her hand and came again. She shook like never before and jumped up on wobbly legs. She tried to make a getaway toward the door.

Prentice caught her and bent her against the dresser. He kicked her feet apart and slid his dick into her from the back. He pulled her long curly hair and got to fucking her like he hated her. Her tight pussy sucked on him like a hungry mouth. He plunged into her forbidden garden and kept hammering away while she knocked a few cosmetics off of the dresser trying to get away from him. He kept going, with no mercy.

Chela somehow wiggled free of him and started to swing wildly. She expected to hit him and knock him out. But Prentice was more of a seasoned fighter than Figgady. He ducked her wild punches. He picked her up and fell to the floor with her. He ripped the top of her gown open and exposed her breasts. Then he was fucking her again, zooming in on her erect nipples. They looked like they belonged on a baby's bottle.

Chela moaned. She held her thighs wide open while he pounded away. She even dared to sit up. When she looked down, she saw his piece going in and out of her box. Her juices leaked to her ass. Prentice pinched her clit and she came again, thrashing about on the floor wildly.

"Mama, where are you?" Chiah asked.

Chela jerked from fear of being caught in the act by her daughter. "Please, Prentice. Let me up. Don't let her catch me doing dis," she hissed.

Prentice growled and forced her to flip over. He pulled her up to her knees and really got to fucking at full speed. "Dis my pussy now. Look, li'l bitch. Yo' mama right hurr." Prentice grabbed her hair into his fist and dogged her out.

Chiah stood by the dresser crying. "Mommy. What are you doing?"

Prentice sped up the pace again. "Awwww shit, bitch! I'm cumming. I'm cumming." He started to jerk into her over and over. They fell to the floor with him on top of her drilling away.

Chela felt him cumming inside of her and groaned. It felt like he was letting loose a water hose of hot water deep inside of her belly. She shuddered and allowed him to finish. She held one finger to her lips for Chiah to calm down.

***

After it was all said and done, Prentice sat Chela down on the couch. He sat across from her with a .40 Glock cocked and pointed at her. Chela held Chiah. She was shaking uncontrollably. She wanted to know what Prentice had in store for her. She hugged her daughter tighter. "Please tell me what you want from me?"

"First of all, send dat li'l bitch to the room, and tell her to close da ma'fuckin' door. Now!" he ordered.

Chela spoke to Chiah in Spanish. She told her that everything was going to be alright. She told her to go back to the room while she talked to daddy's friend. She begged her to.

Chiah reluctantly followed her mother's commands with tears streaming down her face. "Call me when you're done, Mommy. Please," she cried. "You promise?"

Chela wiped tears from her eyes. "I promise."

As soon as Chiah was in the back room with the door locked, Prentice came across the living room and grabbed Chela's arm. "Bitch, be still and don't move."

Chela was already shaking. "What are you doing?"

"Don't worry about it. You just be still and let me take you on a journey." Prentice wrapped a rope around her arm. He took the ready-made syringe full of Sinaloa Tar and injected it into her vein. He made sure that the batch had been extra potent. He knew that if he wanted to find out where Keisha and Mudman were that Figgady was his only hope. He also knew that Chela and Chiah were Figgady's weaknesses. If he got Chela hooked on his poison, then he would run and control her. If he controlled her, then he could control Figgady through her. He pushed the plunger all the way down and fed her the drug.

Chela's eyes rolled into the back of her head. She felt the hot liquid shooting through her veins. Everywhere that it traveled, it felt like it left a soothing feeling of numbness and euphoria. Suddenly her problems didn't exist. Nothing mattered. She felt the beats of her heart slow all the way down. Her eyelids became heavy as cinder blocks. She closed them and smiled. For a moment she forgot about Chiah. She forgot about her issues with Figgady. She even forgot about what had taken place with Prentice. None of those things mattered. All that mattered was the indescribable feeling that she was currently feeling.

Prentice slid beside her and grabbed her jaw roughly. He slapped her face. "Bitch, open yo' eyes. Look at me."

Chela reluctantly opened her hazel eyes and looked into his, squinting. There was music playing in her head that was soothing. She wanted to enjoy it uninterrupted. "What, Prentice?"

Prentice smiled. He stuck his hand between her thighs and inserted a finger back into her gap. Chela tensed and came immediately. The Tar heightened all of her sexual senses. She dug her nails into Prentice's shoulders and moaned into his ear. Prentice liked what he saw. He'd already made up his mind that he was going to spend the next three days giving her as much dope as her body could handle. At the end of the third day, he was sure that he would have full control over her. He tightened his hold on her jaws. "Bitch, listen to me. From here on out, I own you. Do you hear me?"

Chela nodded in and out. The Sinaloa Tar was doing a number on her. She began to snore. Drool dripped from the corner of her mouth. Her eyelids fluttered.

Prentice shook her. "Bitch, wake up."

"What, what, what?" she cried. She frowned and began to sob a bit. "I just wanna be left alone for a minute. Please."

Prentice snatched her up and slapped her face hard enough to get her attention. "Did you hear what the fuck I said?"

She whimpered. "Yes. Yes, please. I heard you."

"And what you got to say about that?"

She nodded out again. She jerked awake before he could say another word. "Okay, dat's cool."

He flung her to the couch and trapped her left arm. "I already know what I gotta do. I got dis. You might be making it seem like you get my drift, but I'ma make sure of dis." He pulled out another syringe and went through the same process as before. His goal was to hook Chela. He had plans on using her to get through to Figgady. His ultimate goal was to find

Keisha and Mudman, and he would do anything to bring that goal to fruition.

Hood Rich

Chapter 8

It was three-thirty in the morning and pouring down raining outside. Lightning flashed across the sky. It was followed by the angry roar of the tropical storm. There was a constant pitter patter on the concrete. Figgady stood on the side of the trap house door with a black, steel Draco in his hands that was stuffed with a magazine that carried a hunnit shots, but he'd been lazy and only loaded ninety bullets. He had two .40 Glocks in the small of his back, and a bulletproof vest across his chest. He straightened the eye holes on his Purge Mask and gave the nod for his li'l homie to smash in the door with the FBI edition battering ram that he'd copped on the low.

Pistol cocked back the ram and slammed it forward into the door as hard as he could. The door busted in. He moved out of the way. He dropped the battering ram and rushed in behind his crew of jack boys. They were met with a full trap house full of hustlers and ghetto bitches, loafing.

Figgady ain't waste no time. As soon as he came through the door, he was busting back to back. The Draco jumped over and over in his hand. He didn't care who he hit, as long as he hit somebody. Niggas, bitches, it didn't matter. He was dealing with some serious depression surrounding the unknown whereabouts of his baby mother Chela and daughter Chiah. He was sure that one of the rival cartels had killed them, and until he found out what took place or where they were, he was going to tear Baton Rouge upside down with no mercy. His first four bullets spit holes through two females. The next six hit three dope boys that were trying to run to the back of the house. They fell to their knees in the hallway. Figgady's hittas ran up on the fallen men and finished them off.

Shots were fired in their direction. Figgady didn't flinch. Instead of him running away from the bullets, he ran toward them, spraying. The Draco spat rapidly. Its bullets flew into the rival shooter's cheeks and dropped him. Figgady stepped over him and kept making his way to the back of the house. He wound up in the kitchen. He looked to his left and saw the pantry door closed. He could hear murmuring on the other side. He nodded with his head at Pistol.

Pistol returned his nod. He stepped back, and then jumped forward, knocking the door in. It flew inward. Pistol let his Mach .90 ride on the people inside. Four more dope boys and two females fell in a heap. Pistol stood over them and kept right on busting. He was from the Ada B. Wells out of Chicago, Illinois. He repped the infamous Bloody 39th Street, a hood known for overkilling their victims. He'd been trained by relentless hittas and he vowed to carry on just like his trainers.

Figgady looked over what he had done with approval. He took the stairs and headed up them. Along the way he kicked in door after door, finding the rooms empty. As soon as he confirmed that there were no more living rivals in the trap, he called for Veronica.

Pistol threw Veronica on the floor in front of Figgady. Veronica was the baby mother of Jax. Jax was the owner and dope boy that ran the trap they were hitting. While fucking, Veronica had made a major mistake and wound up letting her time bump a little bit too much after taking a few pink Mollies, and a Percocet. She told Figgady everything he needed to know about Jax and his trap house. She also told him that Jax was locked up in New Orleans and would be there in their county fighting a murder for she didn't know how long. While he was away, he was having his young crew of hustlers run a few of his traps around the city. Jax was a major dope boy on the south side of Baton Rouge. Figgady planned on hitting every single one of the spots while he was gone.

Figgady grabbed a handful of Veronica's hair and yanked her face to his. "Bitch, whurr you say dat safe at?"

She pointed. "That television right thurr don't work. If you open the side of it, you gon' see a whole bunch of money and dope. Trust me on dat thurr."

Figgady slung her to the floor and stepped over her. He looked over the television and with blazing speed, he punched through the side of it with his black leather gloves. The television exploded. Five bricks of Sinaloa China White fell out of it, along with fifty thousand dollars in cash.

Pistol grabbed a pillowcase and loaded up the spoils. He tossed them to the other hittas, and they disappeared out of the room with them.

"We good, Boss, let's get the fuck out of here."

Figgady grabbed Veronica by her hair and dragged her out of the room. He dragged her down the stairs while she groaned and begged for him to have mercy on her. "Bitch, shut up. We finna go to every spot dis nigga got in dis city and repeat the process. Come on." He threw her on his shoulder.

***

Mudman cracked his knuckles and rolled his head around on his shoulders. He looked across the round table at Miguelito. Miguelito was the first in command of the Bloodthirsty Cartel. He was also Payroll's direct line into Mexico and the plugs down that way. Mudman had ten of Payroll's killas behind him. They were currently honoring Mudman as their head. Each man was armed and ready for war.

Mudman ran his tongue across his gold grill. His eyes were pinned into Miguelito's. "Say, mane, dis how dis shit finna go right now, homeboy. You finna go 'head and give me dat same play dat you was finna give my peoples. I'ma sew up Acorn, City Towers, and Cypress Village. All dem ma'fuckas'll be under me."

Miguelito laughed. He looked behind him to the ten bloodthirsty killas standing on security. They were racist animals. They lived and bled Mexican Pride. "Can somebody please tell me who dis country muthafucka is again? Please." He laughed harder. His killas remained quiet and focused on Mudman and his crew of savages.

Mudman lowered his eyes. He didn't like the cocky Mexican. He hated every tattoo on his face. He hated the smell of his breath, and the scent coming from the apartment building where they were meeting in the basement. In fact, Mudman was just as pro Black as Miguelito was pro-Mexican. Baton Rouge had made him that way.

"Say, esse, I don't know who you are. You just came out of the muthafuckin' blue saying that you're going to be running shit. Don't nobody know you over here. You think it's going to be that easy to take over all of those turfs?"

"Who da fuck gon' stop me?" Mudman could feel his heart beating rapidly. He was getting angry.

Miguelito sneered at him. Something about Mudman gave him an eerie feeling. Maybe it was the pitch black skin. Or maybe it was the gray eyes that freaked him out. Maybe it was because Mudman had been crazy enough to meet him in the heart of the Bloodthirsty Cartel hood. Either way, he needed to figure him out. "Say, homes, what's your deal?"

"Money and power," Mudman said without hesitation.

Miguelito nodded his head. "You think you tough?"

Mudman continued to look him in the eyes. He was seconds away from grabbing his nines and bucking Miguelito down. He didn't give a fuck about dying. Never had. Mudman knew that his time to go was already written in the stars of hell.

Miguelito looked over his shoulder. He had an AK47 sitting on his lap. Under the table, it was aimed at Mudman. His finger wavered on the trigger. "You know who I got ties to, vato?"

Mudman slowly nodded his head. "I wouldn't be sitting hurr if I didn't."

"And you think that you'll be able to handle whatever kind of work that we put in front of you?"

Mudman was silent. He sniffed and pulled his nose. "Acorn, the City Towers, and Cypress Village are all mine."

Miguelito grunted. "Since when? Last I checked, didn't nobody know who you were. The same muthafuckas that were in power last week are still in power, but somehow are these territories yours?"

Mudman laughed. "Muthafucka, I see the future."

Miguelito cracked up at that. "Dis vato is serious. He's really fucking nuts, huh?" He looked around the room. Then he slammed his hand on the table. "Homes, you're in Bloodthirsty hood. We could take yo' life right now, and no muthafucka would care because don't nobody know you out here."

Mudman smiled. He upped both nines and slammed them on the table so hard that the legs of the table cracked inward. All of the men in the room began cocking their guns and aiming them at each other. Mudman remained still. "I want yo' plug, and if I can't get it tonight, then we all about to die in dis muthafucka."

Miguelito remained seated. He mugged Mudman for a long time, then began to nod his head. "Awright, vato, we'll meet in a week. I got a few moves to make, and I'll be back. In the meantime, you take over Cypress Towers. Get that under your wing, and I got some Crystals specifically for that turf. It's what they're used to. Next Friday, if you're the man, I'll supply you with everything that you'll need, and we'll go from there. Deal?" He extended his hand.

Mudman stood up. "Let's go, fellas." He ignored Miguelito's hand and left the basement. Mudman wasn't into faking the funk. He knew Miguelito really didn't like him, and he didn't like him either. All Mudman wanted was his connection to the bosses in Mexico. He would work his way up the ladder however he needed to. His goal was to be the biggest, most successful kingpin that had ever done it, a kingpin that was also a lethal jack boy. Never before had the two been blended. Mudman was dead set on changing all of that.

***

Chela crawled around on the floor, looking for remnants of the Sinaloa. Her head was pounding, and Prentice had been gone for twelve hours. He had her cooped up in his house with Chiah, miserable and waiting for him to return. Her head was pounding. She felt sick, and she yearned for his return. More than once she thought about leaving and running away with Chiah, but she couldn't fathom where she would go. The thought of Figgady looking for her had her so spooked that she dared not step foot outside. Prentice had her cell phone, and she didn't remember any of her other contacts, not that she would have reached out to them anyway. She laid on her side on the carpet and curled into a ball, feeling like she was about to throw up and shit at the same time. The drought of Sinaloa in her system was screwing her over.

Chiah snuck out of the hallway and into the living room. "Mama, are you okay?" she asked, stepping closer.

Chela had the chills. "Yeah, I'm okay, baby. I'm just laying here, dat's all."

Chiah came and laid beside her. She wrapped her little arm around her neck. "I'm hungry, Mama. Ain't we gon' ever eat something?"

Chela was shaking so bad that she couldn't think straight. Suddenly, she didn't want her daughter to be under her. She nudged her away. "Go back to your room, Chiah."

Chiah got up and looked down on her with tears in her eyes. "But I'm hungry, Mama." Chiah hadn't eaten a decent meal in two days. Her stomach growled. She felt faint and extremely dizzy.

Chela came to her feet. "Go to your room, li'l girl, now. I'll bring you some lunch in there later. Now go!"

Chiah ran to the room door and burst into tears. "I hate it here! I want my daddy!"

Chela acted as if she was going to run at her. Chiah rushed into the bedroom and slammed the door just as Chela got there. Chela beat on the door. "You can want yo' daddy, but he don't want nothin to do wit' you. So, get over it!" She beat her fist on the door and walked away from it with her head pounding.

Chiah slid to the floor with her back to the door. She covered her face and cried as hard as she could. She was a daddy's girl. To hear that her father wanted nothing to do with her was almost too much information. She felt like she wanted to die.

Chela made her way back into the living room and collapsed on the floor. She felt weak. Her insides seemed as if they were balling into a knot. "Prentice, where da fuck are you? I need you so bad," she whimpered.

***

Prentice sat in his truck three blocks away watching the footage of his home on his phone. He bit into a double cheeseburger and laughed as he watched Chela squirm on the floor. His plan was coming along nicely. A few more days and he would have her right where he needed her to be.

Chapter 9

Keisha ran across the Mercedes Benz lot from one truck to another. She couldn't seem to make her mind up as to which make and model she was going to cop. She wished she could have parked a truck and a 2020 coupe in front of their new place. She felt spoiled and entitled. The night prior she'd helped Mudman count $300,000 in cash. She'd taken knots of twenty thousand and stuffed them in a duffel bag at his request. Most nights he wouldn't even allow her to help him, but lately he had no problem with it. Keisha knew that he was making money hand over fist, and she felt that since she was his baby that she should have been able to get whatever she wanted.

Mudman held the duffel bag filled with cash on his right shoulder. He had a .45 in the small of his back and a vest across his chest. He stepped beside Keisha and put his arm around her. "Shawty, come on now, which one of dese ma'fuckas you want for yo' birthday?" He staggered a bit on his feet. He was gone off of pink Mollie and two Percocets. In his right hand was a bottle of pure codeine and water. He felt breezy.

Keisha poked out her bottom lip. "I'm saying, daddy, I can't make my mind up on whether I want a truck or that coupe over durr. I wish I could have both." She looked him over from the corner of her eyes.

Mudman smiled. He glanced over his shoulder and saw that his security had all eyes on him. They looked as if they were ready for any blind sides. Another of their cars roamed around the Mercedes Benz lot looking for potential enemies. He was forming an operation that he could be proud of. He looked back down to Keisha. She had on a subtle amount of makeup that enhanced her already natural beauty. Her eyes looked more almond than usual. She smelled like Chanel, and overall, she was his baby. He looked past her and over to the sticker prices. Just by adding a few of the numbers together he figured that two whips fresh off the lot would cost him every bit of eighty thousand dollars. There was a chance that he could negotiate the prices down to about seventy, but even still. He was in a financially building stage. He needed money for his army, his traps, and his arsenal. It would have been foolish to blow eighty G's on whips.

"What are you thanking, baby?" Keisha asked hopefully.

"Since you my ma'fuckin' baby, and you hold a nigga down like nobody else do, you can get whatever you want out dis ma'fucka."

Keisha squealed and ran into his arms. She hugged him as hard as she could. "I love you so much, Rome. You always spoiling me."

He nodded. "You know how dis shit go. Just letting you know though dat I'm 'bout to spin dat nigga on dis lawyer money. He'll get dat shit when I feel like it. So, some backlash might come from it, but I don't give no fucks."

Keisha lowered her eyes. "Fuck dat nigga, daddy. Payroll can get out da best way he know how. He thank he can hold us hostage by saying he gon' go to dem people. Let's just see him do it." She looked coldhearted, staring into his eyes.

Mudman smiled. Her glare made him feel some type of way. He loved when Keisha got on that murder shit with him. It deepened his love and respect for her. "Well, I'm just letting you know." He yanked her to him and tongued her down. He rubbed and squeezed all over her ass, which had gotten considerably fatter ever since they came to Oakland eighteen months prior.

Keisha broke from his embrace. She took off running across the lot. She couldn't believe that she was able to get two vehicles. She felt like it was the greatest day of her life.

***

Figgady nodded at the kitchen table. He scratched his right shoulder before taking a sip from the bottle of codeine. He opened his eyes just a tad so he could see Pistol sitting across the table from him. Pistol was just pulling a syringe out of his arm.

"Say, mane, dis shit hurr fuckin' me up. I miss my daughter, mane. I know one of dese niggas round hurr know where my shawty and her mama at."

Pistol's eyes rolled into the back of his head. He set the syringe on the table and smacked his big lips. "Potna, you already know I'm 'bout what you 'bout. Ma'fuckas might be in Baton Rouge right now, but don't shit but dat Chi shit beat through my veins. Tell me what you wanna do."

Figgady laid his head back and started to snore for thirty seconds. Then he jerked awake and frowned his face. "I'ma turn dis Mafia upside down 'bout mine, mane. Niggas wanna try and attack me from the blind side. Take my shawty and my baby mama. Well, we gon' see bout dat shit thurr. Ain't no hoe in me, Pistol. You already know dat shit thurr." His eyelids became too heavy. He closed them and started to lean forward.

Pistol was snoring now. He scratched at his inner forearm where he had taken his drug. He dug his nails deep to make sure that he got all of the itchiness. It started to bleed, and that felt good to him. "I'm following you, Figgady. We can bring dat Ada B. Wells shit to Baton Rouge, my nigga. If you thank you know who got yo' shawty, den let's go and get her."

Figgady rested his forehead on the table. He nodded. Drool slid out of the corners of his mouth. "Yeah, mane, dat sounds like a plan. I'ma fuck wit' it in a minute. I gotta get dis nodding shit off of me a li'l bit."

Pistol's head was already in his lap and he was snoring away. He jerked back and popped his eyes wide open. He looked around the kitchen and perked up. A natural killa instinct inside of him told him that something wasn't right. "Say, mane, you got our fellas circling the block?"

Figgady nodded his head and scratched his neck. "Always. Dat's what dey get paid for."

"Cool." Pistol nodded back with his head on the table.

All was quiet in the kitchen for five minutes. The steady ticking of the clock on the stove resonated throughout the house. Both Pistol and Figgady snored loudly. A rat pitter pattered across the floor and disappeared behind the refrigerator. The men's snoring grew louder.

Boom! Tissssssssh! Two canisters of tear gas came through the front windows. Boom! Tisssssssh! Three more crashed through the side windows. The lower level of the house began to fill up with smoke. And then gunfire erupted.

Figgady's eyes popped open first. He felt the burning sensation inside of his nostrils. Next his eyes began to burn. The kitchen was being shot up. Big holes appeared in the walls. This windows shattered. He fell to his stomach, and low-crawled into the adjoining room, just as Pistol fell on the floor beside him. Figgady pulled open the bottom drawer of his huge dresser and grabbed his Tech .9 from it. He slammed in a magazine and cocked it.

More bullets ripped through the house. Three more canisters of tear gas bounced against the walls and rolled across the carpet. They stopped and exploded a smoke of pepper spray and Mace-like contents.

Figgady started to choke. He couldn't breathe. He pulled open the back room window and climbed out of it with the Tech .9. Pistol climbed out behind him, and both men took off running toward the alley. Figgady looked both ways and struggled to breathe. His eyes were dripping water off of his chin. He got halfway down the alley and had to stop. His chest felt like his heart was going to explode. He could hear more gunshots ring out. The enemies appeared to be trying to chop down his crib. It made him feel victimized. He felt soft. He felt weak. He couldn't believe that anybody would try to harm him as they had. He wondered if they knew who he was, and what he was capable of.

Pistol pulled him inside of the garage. "Dem ma'fuckas on their way down dis alley, shorty."

Figgady ducked down and watched as two cars sped down the alley and stopped in the back of his house. Four Dominicans jumped out with choppas in their hands. They rushed into Figgady's backyard and began to shoot it up like their comrades in the front. The gun shower lasted a total of five minutes. When sirens were heard in the distance, only then did the attackers scurry off down the alley and away.

Figgady felt perplexed. He could make out a Dominican from anywhere. He also noted the Massachusetts license plates on the backs of both cars. He knew without a shadow of a doubt that Chela's people had tracked him down to the house. Only eighteen months prior, he, Mudman, and Prentice had hit the Dominican Cartel for nearly a million dollars in cash, and over a million in product. He should have known that sooner or later they would come for him. They already had a ten thousand dollar bounty on his head.

Pistol stood up and looked down the alley. "A'ight, the coast is clear. Let's get the fuck out of here before Twelve come. We gotta regroup." Pistol took off running down the alley.

Figgady followed, trying to play over the events in his head. Never before had he been the one that was hunted. He had always been the hunter. The change in roles made him feel weak. He felt sick to his stomach, and knew the feeling wasn't one that he could ever get used to feeling or accepting. It was Murder Season he thought.

***

Prentice slowly pulled away from the curb. He took one last glance at Figgady's house before waving his arm in a circle to give his Dominican hitta the signal. "Blow dat bitch up!"

The Dominican took a step back and threw two grenades inside of Figgady's house. He took off running and jumped into the back of Prentice's rented Explorer. Prentice stepped on the gas. When he got to the end of the block, he heard the explosion. He smiled and drove off the block.

***

Figgady was running at full speed when he heard the explosion. The ground shook under his feet. He stopped and looked over his shoulder. He saw a big cloud of smoke and flames. "What da fuck?"

Pistol eyed the scene with him. He shook his head. "Joe, I don't know what the fuck you did, or who at yo' head, but we gotta knock dey ass off like right away. Come on." He slapped Figgady on the back and they took off running.

Chapter 10

Keisha turned the lights off in the house and knelt down on the pallet that she'd made on the floor. She had lit candles burning all around. She sprayed her perfume in the air and swished her hands around so that it went all over the room.

Mudman stepped out of the bathroom. He was fresh from showering. He walked into the candlelit living room and frowned. "Shawty, what's all dis shit?"

Keisha stayed planted on her knees. She reached out to him. "Come here, baby."

Mudman came to her and knelt down. He wore a pair of pajama pants and a holster. The holsters were filled with his black Glocks. Police edition. He took ahold of Keisha's hands. "What's good, shawty?"

She stepped closer to him and wrapped her arms around his neck. She looked into his gray eyes and felt her heart melt. "I love you, Rome."

"I love you too, shawty. Now turn dese lights on befo' I thank we ain't in dis bitch and try to break in."

Keisha shook her head. "Nall, mane, you don't understand what I'm saying. What I'm tryna tell yo' ass is dat I love you in the highest form of love possible. Rome, I'm ready to die fo' yo' ass wit' no hesitation. I know we ain't got much time left on dis hurr earth, and I don't even give a fuck. When you go, I don't want you to ever leave me behind. Fuck dis world if I ain't got you in it."

Mudman eyed her closely. "Shawty, what's making you say all dis shit?"

She shook her head. "Just my womanly instincts. I feel like we ain't gon' be 'round dis bitch fa too much longer. Figure while we still alive I'll let you know how I'm feeling. Dat's all."

Mudman was silent for a spell. "Shawty, I don't know what you feeling, or what's going on inside of your mind. I just want you to know that you're my baby. I ain't gon' never let nothin happen to you if I can prevent it. You are my first priority. Don't nothing or nobody matter more on dis earth to me than you do. When I go, dat don't mean you gon' go too."

Keisha mugged him. "Don't say dat shit to me, Rome." She ran her fingers through her curly lacefront.

"Fuck you talking 'bout?" He scrunched his face.

Keisha poked him in the chest. "You don't tell me what's gon' happen when you go. I'm telling you right now that I don't wanna be on dis earth if you ain't on it wit' me. You are my sole purpose for breathing. Well, you and my mama. But mostly you. Rome, I don't know why you pursued me so hard, but I'm just glad that you did. I have never been happier in my life." She pulled him to her by use of the back of his neck. She tongued him down, and Mudman returned her affections. "I just love you so much, Rome. You drive me crazy."

Mudman was sucking all over her lips aggressively. He picked her up and laid her back on the pallet. He kissed her some more, pulled his gun out of his holster, and pressed the barrel to her head. He cocked the hammer.

Keisha's eyes got as wide as open windows. She tensed up. "Baby, what are you doing?"

"Bitch, you saying dat when I go dat you gon' be ready to go too. Well, don't you know that I can go at any minute? So, you have any idea how many things wanna take my life right now?" He pressed the barrel harder to her forehead. "Do you?"

Keisha gritted her teeth. She released her hold from his waist. A tear fell from her eye. "Fuck is you waiting on, Mudman? Nigga, you thank I'm scared or somethin'? Huh? Pull dat ma'fuckin' trigger. Kill me den. I ain't scared to die.

If dey gon' take you, den dey gon' take me too. It's as simple as dat. But if you wanna get a jump start, den do it. Do it now!" She raised up and pressed her forehead harder into the barrel.

Mudman grabbed her by the throat. He squeezed. "Dis ain't no game, Keisha. I don't want you in dis ma'fuckin' life, shawty. I almost lost you one time already. I'd never be able to cope if anything ever happened to you. I'd go kamikaze until they killed me."

Tears were spilling down both of Keisha's cheeks. "You can't stop me for riding for you, Mudman. Nigga, you belong to me. You are my man. I'ma ride for you in dis life until it's taken from the both of us. Ain't nobody gon' stop me from riding for you either."

Mudman felt his throat get tight. He wasn't with all that emotional shit. In fact, he believed that real killas didn't have emotions. But there was just something about Keisha. She brought out that sucka nigga side of him, that side that he tried his best to keep it tucked away because it had no place inside of his deadly lifestyle. Keisha was his weakness, his Achilles heel. She was the only one in his life that had conquered a major piece of his black heart.

Keisha wiped her tears away. "So, what you gon' do, Mudman? Huh? You gon' kill me because you love me so much? Huh? You hate to know that yo' crazy ass actually cares about me in the fashion that you do? Dat shit scare you, don't it?"

Mudman slid the gun around until it was resting on her lips. He turned it sideways. "Bitch, shut up. Don't say dat shit."

"Fuck dat. Nigga, you love me. If anyone even thought about touching me you'd kill dey whole family, wouldn't you?"

Mudman started to shake. He imagined somebody hurting Keisha and he nearly blacked out from anger. He got to shaking so bad that it looked as if he was having a seizure. "Don't play wit' me, Keisha.

Keisha took his hand and made him slide the gun into her mouth. She began to give the gun fellatio. She pulled his dick through his pajama hole and opened her thighs wide. "Kill dis pussy, Rome. Fuck me like you love me. Make me yo' bitch like I already am, nigga, or kill me dead," she said around the barrel of the gun. Her speech sounded crazy because of the piece being in her mouth, but Mudman heard everything that she said.

Mudman felt his dick elongate. Keisha rubbed his head back and forth. She slid it past her sex lips and into her steaming hot pussy. Mudman shuddered. He could hear her sucking off the gun, and it was driving him crazy. He got to pounding her out slow at first but fucking as deep as he could. With each stroke she felt better and better.

Keisha moaned around the gun. The taboo of it all drove her crazy. She was truly 'bout that street shit. She loved Mudman because he was a warrior of men. An animal. A legend in his own right. The fact that there was a possibility that their time could be short didn't spook her. What spooked her was the thought of something happening to him, and her not being able to be there to go with him. She opened her thighs wider and deep throated the gun, imagining him pulling trigger.

Mudman took the gun out of her mouth and slid to the side of her. He tossed her right thigh on his shoulder and slid the banger into her cat. He thrust in and out at full speed. "Dis the life we love den, bitch. It's me and you. Us, 'til death."

Keisha looked down, seeing the gun go in and out of her. For some reason, it drove her mad. She screamed and came all over the barrel.

Mudman licked her juices off of it and got between her thighs. He started to fuck her with everything that he had, biting into her neck. "I'll kill for you, Keisha." Thrust after thrust. He pressed her thighs to her shoulders and dug her out, piping her down.

Keisha's eyes rolled to the back of her head. She was in sexual bliss. She couldn't imagine being without him. The thought of it was enough to make her furious with murderous rage. "You ever…leave me… Uh! Uh! Uh! I'll…Shit! Shit! Uhhhhhhhh! I'll kill youuuuu!" she screamed and came hard.

While she shook, Mudman took advantage. He curled her into a ball and got to going crazy in that pussy. When she bit into his neck and drew blood, it became too much. He came, popping his lower back. He could still feel her womb sucking at him.

***

Prentice pulled the hoodie over his head and rang Kimmie's doorbell again. He looked both ways while he stood on the porch. He was higher than a 747. He could feel the Percocets dripping down his sinuses. He swallowed it and straightened himself up a bit before ringing her doorbell again.

Kimmie came to the door with a big cake mixing bowl in her hand. She wiped her face while balancing the phone to her ear. She stepped to the screen door and saw that it was Prentice. "Keisha, I'll call you back. Dat damn boy at my door." She hung up the phone and tossed it on her leather sofa. Then she opened the screen door. "Prentice, the hell are you doing here?"

Prentice smiled. "Damn, Kimmie, don't tell me that you really thank I had somethin' to do wit' Kayla's death?" he said, looking into her pretty brown eyes.

Kimmie was Keisha's mother. She'd watched Keisha and Prentice grow up together from elementary as boyfriend, and girlfriend. When Kayla overdosed off of a hot dose of heroin nearly two years back, Keisha had told her mother that Prentice had been responsible for it. Kimmie didn't know what to believe. Then when she heard that Prentice had been killed, she pushed the entire issue to that back of her mind. "Come to thank about it, son, ain't you supposed to be dead?"

Prentice jerked his head back. "Dang, first I get accused of hurting my li'l sister, somethin' I would never do. Now you saying I'm supposed to be dead? Wow."

Kimmie felt stupid. She wondered if Keisha was just bitter toward him for whatever reason. She didn't know, but she was sure to pick his brain. All she needed was a half hour. She would be able to tell what was what in that amount of time, she was sure of that. "Come on in, baby. We need to talk anyway." She held open the door.

Prentice held the door and allowed her to walk off. He looked down and peeped the way her big booty jiggled under her short skirt. Kimmie had always been fine to him. She was light caramel with brown eyes and a body that would rival any twenty year old stripper's. She kept herself up, and always smelled good. All of the years he was sure that she had been looking at him like a son, and he had been lusting after her gorgeous body. He shook his head at that ass and groaned.

Kimmie set the cake bowl down on the kitchen table and grabbed a ginger ale out of the refrigerator. She took a glass from the cupboard and filled it with ice. She came into the living room with it and set the glass on a coaster. She found Prentice standing in the front room, holding one of the highs school pictures of both he and Keisha. The picture brought back memories.

"I remember dis day like it was yesterday. Dis da same day I bought Keisha that promise rang."

Kimmie laughed. "Yeah, dat damn thang turned that po' baby's finger so green it looked like a piece of asparagus."

Prentice winced and felt offended. He eyed her with anger and forced himself to give her a weak smile. "It was all I could afford back den. I wasn't in dese streets. I wasn't getting that bread like I am now. Now, all I wanna do is spoil her."

Kimmie crossed her arms. "Boy, I thought y'all broke up." Keisha had never told her mother that she was responsible for Prentice's supposed death. She never told her that she had filled his body with slugs. She also never told her that Prentice had basically admitted to killing Kayla. She felt that all of that information would have shattered her mother.

Prentice lowered his head. "We just going through something right now. But that's my baby though. We will always be together. I wanna win her back. Where is she?"

"Dat girl far away from here now, Prentice. She got herself somebody else and she say she happy. I thank you should find yo'self somebody, too. Dat way you can move on wit' ya life and be happy." She handed him the ginger ale.

Prentice took it. Her perfume went up his nose. It aroused him. "Kimmie, you always been like a mother to me, right?"

She nodded and picked up her cake bowl. She got to mixing again. "Sho' have. Ever since yo' mama passed away."

"Right." He stepped into the kitchen. He sized her up. The more she whipped the cake, the more her titties and ass jiggled. He imagined what it would be like to fuck her, and his heart started to pound. The Percocets got to getting the best of him. He moved her hair off of her shoulder and kissed her cheek. "Well, Mama, I wanna know where Keisha is so I can win her back. Why don't you tell me where she is?" He kissed her neck and ran his hand all over her juicy booty.

Kimmie cringed. She set the cake bowl on me table and faced him. "Prentice, what the hell is going on with you?"

He pulled her to him and picked her up. He sat her on the table and got between her thick thighs. He pulled her forward some more so she could feel his pipe. "I always wanted to hit this pussy. I already know you got dat fire."

Kimmie tried to swing at him. "Get off of me, Prentice. It's time for you to leave me house."

"Aw-uh. You just said I was like your son." He snatched her from the table and carried her to her bedroom. He'd always wanted to fuck Kimmie in her bed. As kids, he and Keisha had fucked in it many times before. Oftentimes he imagined that he was fucking Kimmie instead of her daughter. He had a thing for vet women. They intrigued him more. He tossed her on the bed. She scooted backward. Her skirt lifted and exposed her lacy blue panties. "What do you want, Prentice?"

"Where is Keisha?"

"She told me not to tell nobody. I gotta follow my daughter's wishes."

Prentice jumped on the bed and yanked up her skirt. He ripped her panties from her and sniffed the crotch of them hard. Then he tossed them to the floor. "Where is she?"

Kimmie trembled. She felt that Prentice was out of his mind. She watched him take a gun from the small of his back and place his dick head on her opening. "She in California, Prentice. Dat's all I know."

Prentice slammed home. He came as soon as he slid in. Kimmie's pussy was just that good. He shook for a few seconds.

Kimmie felt him splash into her and whimpered. "Get off of me. Please."

Prentice recovered quick. He kissed her lips and sucked all over them. "Where in California, Kimmie?" He held her waist with one hand. Her meaty pussy felt better than both of her daughters to him. "Unnnn, Kimmie. Tell me!" He sped up the pace to a full throttle.

The headboard rocked against the back wall. Kimmie's thighs were wide open. Her cat was taking a pounding from someone whom she deemed to be her son for so many years. She couldn't believe him. She screamed and arched her back. He was fucking her so fast that she couldn't think straight.

"Tell me!"

"Ohhh! Ohhh. Oakland! Oakland! Awwww shiiit!" she screamed.

Prentice pulled her from the headboard and got to bouncing up and down in her. He yanked her shoulder straps down and threw her thighs on his shoulders. "Tell me! Tell me!" he hollered, giving her all she could take.

"I don't know. I don't know where. I don't know!"

"Dat's it!" He pulled out and jumped from the bed. From the inside of his fatigue jacket appeared a shiny hunter's knife. "Before it's all said and done, you gon' tell me everythang." He rushed her.

Hood Rich

Chapter 11

Mudman loaded the hundredth bullet into his magazine. He slammed the clip into his Draco and looked over at Mars. Mars was a dark-skinned, heavyset killa, and second in command at the Acorn Projects before Payroll went down. He had been given direct orders to watch Mudman closely, to make sure that nothing happened to him. He swore his loyalty to Payroll ever since Payroll blessed him into the Game.

Mudman crushed four Percocets and made two lines. He took one to each nostril and coughed. He chased the pills with a swallow from his bottle of codeine. "Say, mane, now you absolutely sho' dey 'bout to be 'bout twenty deep out hurr tonight?"

Mars slammed a clip into his Calico and set it on the table. "Fo' sho'. Two of they homeboys just got released from San Quintin today. I don't know how y'all get down out there in Baton Rouge, but over here in Oakland, when one of yo' homeboys come from under dat slavery, you throw them a nice welcome home party. They been sending out invitations all week. That nigga Pop gon' be there too. You talking about hitting the City Towers crew where it hurts? All we gotta do is hit Pop. He's the head of the snake. Once he falls, the rest of their body gon' follow. Trust me."

Mudman didn't trust a soul. The most he could do was give people the benefit of the doubt. Even then, it seemed a bit much for him at times. "A'ight, now I usually don't fuck with Twelve like dat, but if you thank these hurr suits gon' make dis shit that much easier, then I'm game." He picked up an official police uniform from the Oakland Police Department. "How da fuck you say you got one of dem squad cars again?"

Mars laughed and put on his suit. "Oakland ain't nothing but a big ass price tag. If you got the money, dat brings the clout. Ain't no morals in dis city. Everything is for sale. Trust me when I say everything." He finished getting dressed.

Mudman slipped into the uniform and felt so uncomfortable. He couldn't see how a policeman could wear one of them all day. He especially couldn't understand how they could run in one. He was having a hard time walking in it. "So, what's da plan, shawty?"

"We gon' catch dat nigga Pop before he get to Jackson Park. We gon' hit his ass up right on the street. Gon' allow for one of his boys to get away so dey can call the other homies. Dat should send the park into a frenzy. While they scrambling to get to their cars, bruh n'em gon' heat dey ass up. We got the drop on all of they main hittas and trap stars. We get dem out the way and City Towers belong to Acorn once again. That's money, money, money. Ya feel me?"

Mudman nodded. "Yep. Let's handle dis bidness, homeboy. They li'l get together already done started," Mudman said, looking at his phone.

Mars did the same thing. "Nall, we good. That fool Pop won't move yet. We got a tracker on his car. But still, you right. We should bounce though. Let's get it."

***

Kimmie felt Prentice tie her left wrist to the chair. He had already bound her ankles and right wrist. She was mortified. Prior to the binding, he had fucked her for two hours straight in every hole that she possessed. He had even used her breasts as a tool for his own sexual satisfaction. She still couldn't believe that he was doing all of this to her.

Prentice scooted the chair all the way against the wall and picked his shotgun up from the floor. He cocked it and pressed it up against Kimmie's forehead. "A'ight, Mama. You finna call Keisha and tell her that you wanna come stay with her for a li'l while. Tell her that you already in Oakland and you need her address. Tell her not to argue with you if she tries. Tell her that it's urgent. Do you hear me?"

Kimmie nodded her head. "Okay."

Prentice picked up her phone and searched through her call log. "Dis shit go smooth, and I'ma let you go. I ain't got nothing against you. Just want you to know dat."

"Why did you kill my baby?" Kimmie whispered.

Prentice stopped searching and looked down at her. "What?"

"Kayla? Why did you get my daughter hooked on that stuff? Why did you kill her? The autopsy report said that she had taken a dosage of heroin potent enough to kill a grown elephant. They said somebody purposely gave her that dose. That her usage was new. Keisha told me that you had something to do with it, but I never believed her for one second. But guess what? I do now."

Prentice frowned. "Bitch, we ain't got time to get into to all of dat. Kayla dead, and life goes on. We finna take care of dis situation right hurr and be dome wit' it. Now like I said, if she gets to asking you a whole bunch of questions, you tell her you'll let her know when you get dere."

"I ain't doing shit till you tell me why you killed my baby. She had a future. She had scholarships. You took all dat away from dis family! Why would you do that when we were so good to you, Prentice! Why!" she snapped.

"Bitch, ask Keisha that muthafuckin' question. Ask dat bitch why she run off to California with my cousin, after she tried to kill me? Ask dat bitch why she cheated. She's responsible for Kayla's deaths, not me."

Kimmie shook her head. "Everybody is responsible for their own actions. At some point in your life, you have to man up and admit what you've done. You took my baby away from me."

Prentice grabbed a handful of her hair and yanked her head sideways, causing her neck to pop. It hurt so bad that Kimmie couldn't help screaming out in pain. She could literally feel something poking at the skin surrounding her neck. "Bitch, we finna call Keisha. We gon' get dis address, and you gon' go on 'bout yo' bidness. It's as simple as dat. Here we go." He released his fingers from her hair and started to dialing.

"You thank I'ma let you kill another one of my kids? Satan, I rebuke you in da name of Jesus!" she screamed.

Prentice grew angry. "Bitch, what is you saying?"

"I'm telling you to go to hell where you belong! Yea, though I walk through the shadow of death, I fear no evil. Thy rod and thy staff comfort me. I - " She chanted.

Prentice balled his face. "Shut up, bitch! Shut up!" He stood back and aimed his shotgun at her face and pulled the trigger.

Kimmie saw the bright flash. Then she felt the hardest punch she'd ever felt in her life. It burned into her eye and flew out the back of her head. She felt her brains melt onto her the left side of her collar. She fell backward in the seat.

Prentice stood in front of her and unloaded all five rounds. He left Kimmie's body tied to the chair. Her head had been completely taken off of her neck. The basement looked like a can of paint exploded. Prentice stood over her for a long time, pissed. It had been a blank mission. Once again, he was right back where he started.

***

Mudman hit the switch to emit the sirens on the police car. He had Pops's Range Rover in front of him and needed to seize the moment. Mars shone the big spotlight on the back of the truck to slightly blind the driver in case he tried to get away.

Pops cursed under his breath. He took the .9 millimeter and slid it into the console deep enough so that it wasn't visible. He looked over to his li'l brother. "Dese muthafuckas always fuckin' wit' somebody. Sons of bitches."

He brother nodded and looked into the back of the truck at the two thick females they had picked up from Acorn. He had plans on fucking both of them, but most especially the dark-skinned goddess. She was super strapped to him. He had to see what that was about. He handed her his dope and .40 Glock.

"Shawty, put dis here in yo' purse. Dem law can't fuck wit' you. I got two strikes. They can give me life. Worse comes to worst, you need bail. I'll take care of dat, don't even trip. A'ight?"

"Yeah, daddy, dat sound cool to me?" she responded, tucking away his contraband.

He laughed. *I love dumb hoes,* he thought.

Mudman slowly walked to the driver's side of the car with his hand over his service holster. Inside it, he was strapped with a Glock .9. He held the flashlight in his other hand. "Driver, I'ma need you to turn off the car. Show me your hands."

Pops rolled down the window just enough. "Man, why da fuck you pigs fucking wit' me? Huh? Ain't y'all got shit else better to do?" he hollered.

"Turn off the ignition and put your hands where I can see them. Drop your keys out of the window," Mudman reiterated.

"Dese pigs on something, man. Dey must know about dem shootings from two days ago. Man, fuck dat, I ain't going back to San Quentin. They gon' have to kill me first," Pops said, grabbing his gun from the console. "James, I'm finna kill his ass and you hit his partner," Pops ordered.

"Nigga, you serious?" James inquired.

"As a heart attack." Pops slid his pistol into his lap.

James, seeing that he was serious, demanded his gun back from the dark-skinned sister in the back. "Shawty, let me get that." He reached his hand out for her to place his gun in it.

"I repeat. Turn off your ignition and drop your keys out of the window!" Mudman hollered.

"Man, fuck dis!" Pops rolled his window all the way down with the intentions of murdering the man in blue. He stuck the nose of his gun out of the window. "Hey, Pig!"

Boom! Boom! Boom! Boom!

Pops felt the bullets punch him in the back of his head. His eyes were still opened when his brains splattered across the front windshield. He fell face first on the steering wheel, causing it to blare loudly.

"Man, what the fuck!" James hollered, shocked.

Keisha turned her gun on James and finger fucked it nine times, blowing him all over the passenger's seat while some bitch that she didn't know screamed in her ear. "Nigga, that's for calling me shawty. And bitch, shut up!" she hollered.

Mars slid to the side window and yanked open the back door. He pulled the woman out by her hair and pulled her to him. "Bitch, you got some of dem nigga's phone numbers that's gon' be at the welcome home party?"

She nodded. "Yes. Please don't hurt me."

Mars slapped her across the face. "Call dem and tell dem dat Pops and James just got murdered. Go!"

She took off running, dialing her phone at the same time. She called her best friend, then her brother and his baby mother. She screamed that it just happened.

Mudman looked down on Keisha. He grabbed her by the shirt and brought her at full speed to his lips. He tongued her down? "A'ight, boo, go finish dat bitch."

Keisha took off running in pursuit of the woman. She ran for a block and half. She found her sitting on somebody's porch steps, crying her eyes out.

Keisha slid up. "Bitch, peek a boo."

She looked up. "What?"

Boom! Boom! Boom! Boom! Boom!

Mudman pulled the cruiser to the curb. He watched Keisha lean down and check the pulse of the woman before she jogged to the cruisers and got into the back seat. "Let's get over to dis park. Ma'fuckas gotta be in a frenzy.

***

Mudman sat on the windowsill of the Police Cruiser, along with Mars on the opposite side, both bucking from their fully automatic weapons. Keisha drove through the grass of the park. It was pure mayhem. All of Mudman's troops joined in on the action as they bucked their Draco's and Tech. 9s. Members from the City Towers returned fire, but they were overpowered and outgunned. It sounded like a fireworks show. The night lit up as Mudman's crew popped their guns. It lasted for all of three minutes, but it was enough time to leave behind twenty bodies. Mudman rolled away from the scene, thirsty for more blood. He was becoming addicted.

Chapter 12

It was three days after the massacre of the enemies that resided in the City Towers. Mudman adorned another disguise. He sat at the jail phone window, waiting for Payroll to enter into the visit. The visiting area smelled like heavy cheap perfume. Mudman looked to his left and saw a heavyset woman with her breasts pulled out. She squeezed them together and breathed huskily into the phone, "Get it, baby. Yeah, show me dat you miss me." The heavyset woman ran her tongue across her lips and played between her thighs. Mudman shook his head. He turned back to the glass just as Payroll sat down and picked up the phone.

"Look, nigga, I ain't tryna hear shit. You betta have that first fifty or we finna have a serious problem," Payroll threatened.

Mudman played it off. "Chill, li'l nigga. I got dat bread for you. Where you want me to put it, on yo' books or somethin'?" he asked, knowing damn well he couldn't do that.

Payroll's eyes lit up. "Nigga, you got the whole fifty thousand? Seriously?"

Mudman nodded. "What you want me to do wit' it?"

Payroll was caught off guard. "Damn, look. I'ma get in touch wit Justin Bivens again. As soon as he tell me where he want da money sent, we gon' be on and popping. Until den, I need you to put some money on my J Pay." J Pay was how inmates had money sent to their accounts on the inside. The fact that Mudman had told Payroll that he'd finally raised enough money to make the first payments to acquire an attorney, and Payroll was still asking for money to be placed on his books, told Mudman that Payroll was greedy and a bit ungrateful.

"Mane, I just sit hurr and told yo' ass dat I came up wit' dis scratch to help you get Justin Bivens, and you still gon' be greedy an ask me for money for yo' books? Nigga, what's wrong wit' you?"

Payroll took his ear away from the phone and looked at the receiver. He was offended. He placed the phone back to his ear and mugged Mudman through the glass. "Potna, who da fuck you think you talking to?"

Mudman eyed him in silence. He balled his hands into fists. He had an utter disdain for Payroll. He didn't like anything about him. He knew he wasn't tough. If it came down to it, Mudman would break every bone in his body if he had the chance to. He clutched the phone in his right hand so hard that it stared to crack.

"Nigga, until I get back out there, you working for me. That's how that shit finna go. Don't be sitting yo' ass over there thinking that you some major nigga right now because you ain't doing shit but moving through my city, with my clout. If I say I want you to put some money on my books after you got me an attorney, then that's just that, period." He wiped his mouth. "Now I need like a G. Make that shit happen!" He hollered the last part into the phone.

Mudman continued to glare at him. He imagined chopping him up into little both pieces and force feeding him to Payroll's mother. He couldn't wait for him to get out so he could beat him senseless. Mudman nodded his head. Since he had no intentions on dropping the fifty thousand dollars for Justin Bivens, he figured he would buy time by placing a G on his books. "A'ight, li'l homie. I'm finna send you dat G as soon as I step out of hurr. Den I'ma hit up Justin Bivens's office first thang in the morning. We gon' get you up out of hurr." Mudman tried his best to not curl his lip. He didn't want to show any signs that all he was thinking about was killing Payroll in a sadistic fashion.

Payroll sucked his top row of teeth and ran his tongue over them. "Now that's more like it. A ma'fucka can't be looked at as no boss in dis bitch if I can't even make canteen. Fuck type of shit is dat?"

Mudman smiled weakly. "Yeah, I get it, and I got you, homeboy."

"Another thing. I heard how you handled the City Towers run. That's what's up. When I come out of here maybe you can sit a few seats under me. We could handle some supreme bidness."

Mudman laughed at that. Then he played it off. He didn't have that worker shit in him. He would never work for, or under, any man. He was against it. Mudman was a born leader. A king. Head. When he looked at Payroll, all he saw was a peasant. A pussy. A sheep inside of a wolf's costume. Mudman was all wolf. All the time. "Yeah, we gon' see 'bout dat, mane. Anyways, let me get up out of hurr." Mudman rose to get up when Keisha appeared in the walkway that led to the exit. He mugged her. "Fuck you doing up hurr, shawty."

She looked stunning with her silky black hair highlighted with gold streaks. She wore a pair of Chanel gold-rimmed glasses, and the matching skirt and suit coat. She lit up the area with her rich perfume. Keisha looked like she was worth a million dollars, an felt like it as well. "I wanna talk to him."

"Who, dat nigga?" Mudman asked, leaning out of character. He didn't like Keisha talking to no nigga. He didn't give a fuck if it was her cousin or not.

"Yeah, I just gotta feel his ass out and see somethin'." She walked over to Mudman and grabbed the phone from his hand.

Mudman mugged her for a second. He wanted to snap. He wanted to pop her for getting out of their truck. He wanted to say so much. Instead of losing his cool, he walked off. "I'll see you in da truck, shawty."

She rolled her eyes and did it purposely so Payroll could see her. She looked him over and smiled. "Hey cuz."

Payroll nodded with his eyes bucked. "Damn, Keisha, you look good as a muthafucka. You got me over here thinking about all kinds of crazy shit. You lucky you my cousin." He could smell her perfume on his side. Her supple breasts were bunched together in her top. The swells looked delectable. They were chocolate and shiny. He felt his piece rising. He squeezed it. "Dat nigga getting on yo' nerves, huh?"

Keisha opened her jacket just a little bit, so her globes were more exposed. She was wearing a push-up bra, and her D cup breasts were really spilling out of it. She crossed her thick thighs and pulled back her skirt three inches. Her flesh was nicely displayed. "Nall, he just being him. I'll be glad when yo' ass get out though."

"Who you telling? How you holding up out there though?" he asked, trailing his eyes down to her cleavage.

Keisha peeped him. She played it off as if she didn't though. "I'm doing good. Taking shit one day at a time. Making sho' yo' old lady got everythang dat she need. Yo' stepdaughter too."

"Dat's what's up." He squeezed his piece and tried his best to not allow for the sight of her to affect him. He was struggling. His piece stood up straight along his stomach. He shifted uncomfortably. "Look, we ain't got dat much time. What brings you down here to see me?"

Keisha nonchalantly eased her skirt up. She arched her back and uncrossed her thick thighs and spaced them. She was sure that he could see almost up to her cat. She was without panties for a reason. "I wanna know how you finna play dis shit you in hurr for. My old man say he get the inkling dat you might be leaning toward putting dat shit on little ole me. You wouldn't do something like dat now, would you?"

Payroll leaned his head back. He was trying as best he could to see up her skirt. He was feening to see. Never in his life had he ever looked at Keisha in the context, but now he was seeing her in a whole new light. His dick was throbbing like crazy, and he couldn't think straight. "I just said dat shit because yo' ole man was acting like he was gon' leave a nigga stranded in dis bitch. Dat shit would have been fucked up. So, I said what I said to light a fire under his ass. I ain't mean dat shit doe. Ain't no rat in me."

Keisha rubbed her inner thigh. "You sho' 'bout dat?"

Payroll slid his hand into his pants and started to stroke his piece brazenly. He was feening for some pussy. He didn't give a fuck where he got it from. "Damn, Keisha, you fucking my head up right now. You should know I would never get down on yo' li'l fine ass like that."

Keisha spread her legs all the way apart. Now she was sure that he was looking at straight pussy. She pulled the lips together and moved her hand out of the way. "I need you to get up out of there so me and you can begin understanding. I need you out here wit' me, cuz. Dat's why I came back to Oakland. Did you forget?"

Payroll was working himself as fast as he could. He saw the dew on her chocolate lips. The way it slightly flashed her pink. Her thick thighs, which were smooth. The scent of her. And the fact that he knew he wasn't supposed to be doing what he was doing. All of it became too much for him. "Keisha, rub that ma'fucka. Please. Hurry up, rub dat ma'fucka."

Keisha squeezed her sex lips together and rubbed her middle fingers up and down her crease. As she slid both fingers into herself and moaned into the phone. "Payroll! Uh!"

He came all over his fist, jerking, and groaning. His stomach muscles clenched over and over. He squeezed the excess into his shirt and started to wipe his piece clean.

Keisha pulled down her skirt. She fixed her blouse. "Payroll, when you get up out of there, you and I need to go away for a trip or something. We need to get better acquainted. What we gon' do ain't gon' be nobody bidness but our own. Can you promise me dat?"

He nodded. He felt weak and disgusted with himself. Even so, when he imagined what a trip would be like with him and Keisha doing shit that they knew they weren't supposed to be doing, it excited him. "You gotta make sho' you stay on yo' nigga's ass for me. I done supplied him with everythang that he needs to advance in dem streets. He shouldn't have no excuses."

Keisha nodded and smiled. "On some real shit, dat nigga want you out here more than I do. He hit that trap every day to hustle for you," Keisha lied. "He know you mean bidness. I be telling him dat you ain't da one to play wit."

Payroll felt superior. "A'ight den. I guess I can give his ass a li'l space to do what he need to den?"

"Yeah, I'm on top of it, cuz. Oh, and I'ma personally holler at Justin Bivens for you. He supposed to be in meetings all dis week and up to Wednesday of next week. But as soon as he get back, I'ma pull up on him and convince him to take your case." Keisha was lying her ass off. She just needed to buy time so Mudman could do what he needed to do in order to conquer Oakland before Payroll got wise to them. As far as Keisha was concerned, Payroll was a dead man walking. She wanted to spit in his fucking face. Showing him her charms was just a means to hook him and reel him in. It had been all Mudman's plan, and it seemed to be working like a charm. She placed her hand on the glass. "I love you, cuz, and I'm riding for you. Always know dat. You're my heart." She almost wanted to puke after uttering those words.

"You mines too, baby. Just handle yo' bidness, and what should I do?" he asked. The guard came and stood over him, letting him know that his visit was over.

"You just hold ya head up. I'ma make sure some money get put on yo' account. And first thang Wednesday, I'm in Attorney Bivens's office. Dat's my word."

Payroll molded his hand on the glass to cover hers. "A'ight, cuz. Come holler at me a week from today. I'ma schedule it."

***

When Keisha got outside Mudman was banging Kevin Gates. He nodded his head and turned down the music. He jumped out and opened her door for her. "Everythang is everythang, shawty?"

Keisha laughed. "He came. I knew that nigga was on some other shit wit' me. But yeah. We got some time to do what we need to do. You put some chump change on his books, and let's keep doing us. We got dis."

Mudman closed her door. He loved his bitch. She earned that love. For Keisha, he would smoke a million ma'fuckas wit no regard. He sat in the driver's seat and unzipped his pants. "Shawty, suck on daddy, and tell him what just took place."

Keisha shivered. "I got you."

***

Prentice bit into the Southern Fried Chicken that Marjorie had prepared for him. He drenched it in tabasco sauce and felt his stomach rumble for the third time. "Man, dis that work right hurr, Aunty." He bit into the drumstick again and ripped the meat from the bone. He grabbed the blue Kool-Aid that he'd mixed with an eighth of Codeine. He downed half of the cup.

Marjorie sat tied to the chair. Tears ran from her eyes. She didn't understand what was going on. She was wishing that she had never let her sister's son into her home. "Prentice. What is all of dis about?"

Prentice sucked his fingers. He spooned big portions of macaroni into his mouth and chewed, smacking all loudly. "I came over hurr to get some of dis good-ass cooking. Dat's it, dat's all." He ripped meat from a thigh of fried chicken and began to smack some more.

Marjorie whimpered. "Boy, why am I tied to dis chair?"

He looked over at her and laughed. "Oh, dat." He ate some more of his food.

Marjorie looked him over as if he was out of his mind. "Well?"

"You tied up 'cause I don't like people moving round me while I'm eating. Where is Rome?"

Marjorie froze. "Why are you looking for my son?"

"Dat's neither here nor there. Where is he?" Prentice got up and took a knife out of the knife holders and sat back down. "I'm listening.

Marjorie closed her eyes. " I don't know what's going on, or what's gotten into you. My son's bidness is his bidness. You wanna know where he at, you ask him. Now untie me," she demanded.

Prentice knocked the plate of food off of the table and flipped the entire table. He grabbed her shirt into his fist and cocked back the knife. "Where is he?"

"I ain't scared of you, Satan. All of my sins have been forgiven. I'm ready to go, so kiss my ass."

"Bitch!"

Marjorie felt the knife plunge into her throat. It sliced through her vocal cords and caused a spilling of blood to rush into her throat. She kicked her legs. The pain was immediate. Prentice went ballistic and stabbed her over and over until he grew out of breath. Then he pushed over her chair and fell to his knees.

"Mudman! Keisha! I'ma kill you muthafuckas! I swear!" he hollered in his obsession over the pair.

Chapter 13

Chela pulled the platinum Lexus truck in front of Figgady's trap and cut the ignition. She took the keys out and looked herself over in the mirror. She'd applied enough makeup. She prayed that he wouldn't be able to tell that she was strung out. She opened the driver's door and walked up and knocked on it.

Two of Figgady's security ran around the sides of the house at blazing speed. They jumped the porch and one of them snatched her up while his partner held her at gunpoint. "What da fuck you want, shawty?" the gunman asked in a harsh tone of voice.

Chela threw her hands up and held them at shoulder length. "Hey, chill out. I'm looking for my baby daddy, Figgady. I need to talk to him," she said, looking from one man to the next.

The one holding the gun mugged her with hatred. "Bitch, what's yo' name?"

"Chela. I'm his daughter's mother. If he's in there, can you please tell him that I need to speak to him?"

The gunmen looked her over. He didn't know if she was telling the truth or not. He was fresh from Chicago. He knew that Figgady had a bunch of enemies in Baton Rouge. Chela could have easily been a female that was trying to set his big homie up. Chicago was well known for having the women in the cliques set up men before they met their demise. It was the Windy City way. "Shawty, my homie gon' take you around to the back door. I'ma go in here and see if Figgady knows who you is," he lied.

"Okay." Chela looked over to his homie.

"Bruh, Figgady say he gon' be gone for a few hours. He ain't in there right now."

The gunman looked him over as if he was stupid. "So what? Dis bitch going inside anyway." He looked Chela up and down and saw how the skirt was fitting her right. She looked foreign to him. Her accent had him feeling some type of way. Figgady had never said anything about having a baby mother since he had been in town. He was sure that Chela was trying to run script on him.

Now Chela was nervous. She saw the look in both men's eyes and decided against going inside with them. "You know what? That's okay. I'll just come back at another time. Maybe I'll try his phone first." She started to back away.

Now the gunmen felt that she really was lying about being Figgady's baby mother. If she was, he wondered why she had not called him to begin with. "Bitch, you got the game fucked up. Now you ain't got no other choice. You going with us, and that's just that." The gunman grabbed a handful of her hair and yanked her to him.

Chela yelped. "Please, I just came over here to talk to my baby daddy." She struggled to get away from him.

The other teen swung and connected with her jaw. "Bitch."

She slumped to the ground, out cold. Her face was planted against her chest. Though she was asleep, a part of her could feel the blood from her nose dripping off of her lip.

The gunman tucked his gun. "We got dis bitch. Come on, help me get her inside."

***

Savanna opened the door and lit up when she saw Keisha's face. "Hey cousin."

"Hey baby, whurr is yo' mama at?" Keisha asked, hugging her.

"She in the kitchen. I think something is wrong with her."
Keisha frowned. "You sure?"

"Yep. You gon' see." She closed the door and locked it.

Keisha walked into the kitchen, and noticed Sandra sitting there with her head down. She could her whimpering. She slid beside her and rubbed her back. "Hey girl, what's wrong?"

Sandra shook her head, and wiped tears from her eyes. "I'm sick of dis shit, Keisha. I can't take it no more."

"What's the matter?" Keisha asked softly.

"All dis shit. These projects. The lifestyle. The bills. Waiting on him to get his shit right. All of it is too much for me. It's killing me."

Keisha nodded in understanding. "Girl, you should know that you're not alone though. I know it's hard, but anything you need help with, you know that me and Mudman are here for you and your children." She kissed her cheek.

Sandra sighed, and smiled. "I know that. I appreciate that. I just want better. I'm tired of being in this hell hole. Oakland ain't getting no better. The crime is getting worse. It's more and more murders every single day. Every time I walk out of this apartment I'm always worried about somebody doing something to me because they wanna get back at my man. On top of that, we're so far in debt that it don't make no sense. I'm just sick of it. Now dis boy telling me that he need me to come up with fifty thousand dollars so I can help y'all get him a lawyer faster. Where the fuck am I going to get some cash like that? The only thing that we have remotely close to that is his life insurance policy." She lowered her head again and kept it there while Keisha rubbed her back.

Keisha had all types of things running through her head. She wanted to get rid of Payroll once and for all. She had taken a liking to both Sandra and Savanna, and she didn't want to hurt them. On the other hand, it seemed like Sandra was over their relationship. The devious side of her kicked in. "Girl, how much is his life insurance policy for?"

"Two hundred thousand. Why you ask me that?" Sandra wanted to know.

"Oh, I was just wondering." Keisha continued to rub her back some more. "Just curious. If you were to leave Oakland, where would you go?"

"Back home to Los Angeles. Crenshaw, or Baldwin Hills. One of the two."

"Aw, well, if I was you I would be looking to be up out of Oakland soon anyway. You're right, Payroll does have a lot of enemies. One of them could easily take that shit out on you, or one of your children. That wouldn't be fair. He got a lot of fighting to do wit' those charges he got. Ain't no telling how long it's gon' be before he is back out."

Sandra agreed. "Yeah, I guess. Keisha, Payroll said that you're the one that killed Cartier. He said that he is taking the rap for you. Is that true?"

Keisha felt her blood run hot. She frowned at Sandra. "Girl, hell n'all, dat ain't true. I don't know what would make him say something like that. But whatever. I'm not gon' let dat concern me. What I need for you to do is to get your household in order. Y'all get ready to move back to Los Angeles until Payroll comes from out of there. Me and Mudman will help you with the expenses. Okay?"

Sandra hugged Keisha. "Girl, I love you so much. You are the one good thing that has come from Payroll. You, Mudman, and my son."

Keisha's eyes were low and conniving as she looked over Sandra's shoulder to the picture of Payroll sitting on her living room table. "You never know, girl. As crazy as shit is on the inside, anything could happen to Payroll. I mean, God forbid. But if it did, at least you'd have two hundred thousand dollars to grieve with." Keisha imagined slicing Payroll's throat. She even saw the blood pour out of it and run down his chest. That made her smile.

Sandra didn't know how to respond to what Keisha had just said. "Girl, let me go and make a few calls, and I'll let you know what I'ma decide." She broke her embrace with Keisha and stood up.

Keisha dusted off her Prada 'fit and picked a piece of lint off of her skirt. "Okay den. Girl, just make sure you let me know what you thanking so I can get you right. I don't know if you should bombard Payroll with all of that, but if you do...Well, good luck."

***

"Nigga, ain't nobody fuckin' in our bidness. Tell me how one crew can shut down a whole side of town?" Pistol jacked.

Figgady kept rolling his Benz truck. He searched the streets for potential enemies. He was high as a star, his eyes low as a sewer. "What a ma'fucka gotta do to put dat food on da table. I gotta make sure my dogs are eating. Dat's what dis shit is all about." He was itching badly. He scratched his inner forearm and licked his dry lips.

Pistol scanned the dark streets. "Baton Rouge sweet though, nigga. We would have never been able to do none of dis shit in Chicago. Ma'fuckas back home playin' fa keeps. Dese country niggas out here get everythang late. They also sleep on our tactics. I thank dat's why we been so successful so far. "

"Nall, nigga, we been so successful because I'm sitting in the driver's seat. As long as I'm calling the shots, we gon' be in the best possible position. That's on me, my nigga." Figgady adjusted the AK47 on his lap. He saw a billboard for

Pampers as he rolled down the busy Martin Luther King Street and across the tracks. For some reason it made him think of Chiah. He missed his daughter. It had been two months. He wondered why Chela avoided his calls. He wondered why she hadn't reached out to him. He hoped that they were okay. Most importantly, he hoped that they were still alive.

Pistol rubbed his face with his hands. "Joe, I'm hungry as a bitch. Let's stop at one of these restaurants and get somethin' to eat."

Figgady nodded and kept rolling. He had two duffel bags of cash on his back seat. He needed to get him and Pistol back to his safe house so they could count the bags of money that they had come on after hitting a week worth of Kick Does.

Figgady pulled into Jack in the Box, and rolled up through the drive thru, where they ordered their food. He paid, and they pulled around to the second window to pick up their food.

"Mane, we gotta brang some more of the homie from the buildings down to Baton Rouge. Dey gon' love how sweet it is." He sparked a blunt and started to smoke.

The Asian girl handed Figgady his bag of food and he pulled off. As he was rolling out of the parking lot, Prentice was rolling into it. They locked hate-filled eyes with one another. Figgady kept rolling. He felt his blood go cold. "Bitch-ass nigga," he mumbled.

Pistol sat up alertly. "Fuck you talking 'bout? Who?"

Figgady nodded with his head at Prentice's Benz. "Prentice's punk ass. I just seen him turn into the drive thru."

"What, you want me to go sweat his ass?" Pistol cocked his Mach. 90 and looked out of the window. He spotted Prentice's Benz and grew angry.

Figgady thought about it for a moment. A part of him wanted to let Pistol jump out and wet him. Then he thought about all of the money he had in his truck and decided against it. He would run into Prentice again. Baton Rouge was small. "Nall, mane, we gon' get up wit dat fuck nigga at another time. Believe dat."

Pistol continued to mug him. "A'ight den. Well, when you ready to feed dat nigga to the morgue, you already know all you gotta do is say da word."

"When it's time, I'ma handle dat nigga myself. Dis is personal. Come on, let's get to the trap."

***

Chela felt the gunman fucking her as hard as he could from the back. His homie forced her to go down on him. They had already switched positions twice. She felt sore and sick to her stomach. She felt the gunman tense up, and then he was pulling out his piece nutting all over her ass. He groaned and stroked his piece.

Chela heard a door slam. Then voices. She pulled her mouth off of the one in front of her and tried to swallow her spit. As soon as it was down her throat, she screamed. She screamed as loud as she could. "Help me! Help me!" She didn't care if the voices she heard were only going to hurt instead of help her. She decided to roll the dice.

"Shut up, bitch." The one that was in front of her grabbed her by the throat and began to choke her as hard as he could with two hands.

"Kill dat bitch. Kill her!" the gunman hollered.

Chela kicked her feet wildly. She couldn't believe that this was happening to her. She thought about Chiah as the choking intensified.

Figgady bust through the room door and looked down on the scene. Chela was butt naked with cum all over her. His young hitta was between her thighs with his pants pulled down to his ankles. His other young homie was butt naked. It took him a second to grasp what was taking place in front of him. When it all clicked into his psyche, he snapped. He removed the one between her thighs. He yanked him off of her and threw him into the wall. Then he turned around and grabbed the other one by the neck. He lifted him up in the air and slammed him on the floor as hard as he could, knocking him out. He went back to the other one and pistol-whipped him for five whole minutes. When he was done with him, his skull was caved in. The carpet was a bloody mess. Then he finished off the other one the same way. After he caved in his skull, he stood up and stomped both of their faces in over and over again.

Chela crawled into a corner and curled into a ball. "They're dead, Figgady. They're dead already. Baby, stop. They are already dead," she cried.

Figgady didn't stop for another few minutes. Then he looked down on them with his chest heaving up and down. He turned to Chela. "How did dis happen? How?"

"I came looking for you, and they did this to me. I missed you. I needed you."

Figgady snatched her up and slung her into the wall. Where the fuck is Chiah, bitch? Where is my daughter?" he snapped.

"I can't tell you that," she cried. "Please don't make me."

Figgady backhanded her with no remorse. She fell to the floor. He picked her back up and held his forearm under her chin. "Where the fuck is my daughter, bitch?"

"She's with Prentice. He wants to talk to you. He got our baby, and he say he gon' kill her if you try anything stupid. Dis is all my fault," she cried.

Figgady grabbed her by the hair. "Come on, bitch. We going over there right now. Pistol, get in here and clean up dese niggas. Throw they asses in the creek and get this room in order. I'll be back."

Chapter 14

Figgady stepped to Prentice's front door and beat on it as hard as he could. He held Chela's hair tight in his fingers.

Prentice had already seen Figgady pull up. He smiled and sent his troops outside to meet both him and Chela on the porch. She was dressed in a long trench coat. Prentice's paranoia made him think that Figgady had fitted her in bombs of some sort. He tucked his. 45s into their holsters and made his way down the steps. He waited at the front door.

Figgady saw the two killas run along the side of the house. They hopped the porch and rushed him. Before he could react, he was being held at gunpoint. He didn't pay them any mind. He beat on the door some more. "Prentice, open dis ma'fuckin' door so we can talk!" he ordered.

Prentice downed the rest of his codeine and unlocked the door. "Nigga, bring yo' bitch ass in. Carry dat hoe wit' you."

Figgady rushed inside and threw Chela to the floor. He wound up nose to nose with Prentice. "Where the fuck is my daughter?"

Prentice kept his silence. He could smell the Lean on Figgady's breath. It pissed him off. He felt like grabbing one of his .45s and blowing him away but decided against it. His war wasn't with Figgady. It was with Keisha and Mudman. Figgady was just the middleman. Yet if he had to kill him in order to get to them, he would have no problem doing that. "Seems like we both got somethin' that the other one wants, don't we?"

Figgady pressed his forehead against his. He was seeing red. He was thinking murder in the most sadistic fashion. Nobody played with his child. Nobody. "Nigga, you got five seconds to tell me where my baby is. If you don't, you finna have to kill me right here, and right muthafuckin' now."

Prentice smirked. "Nigga, calm yo' ultra-black ass down. Her li'l ass awright. I wouldn't lay a finger on yo' li'l girl unless you made me do it. I just want some information. That's all."

"Ain't no snitches over here, nigga. Rats get bodied. It's as simple as dat!" Figgady snapped. He eyed Prentice with extreme hatred.

"Nigga, fuck what you talking 'bout. I need to know where Mudman and Keisha are right now. I'm tired of playing dese games with everybody in dis city. Tell me where dey at? Now, muthafucka, or lose your daughter."

"What?" Figgady snapped.

"Man." Prentice pushed him as hard as he could. Figgady went falling backward. Prentice upped both .45s and aimed them at the 6'4" giant. "Fuck you thought dis was? Nigga, you betta tell me what I need to know, or I'ma blow yo' ass back."

Figgady flew into the wall and bounced off of it. He stood beside Chela. He pulled a .9 millimeter off of his hip and got ready to aim it at him.

"Noooooo!" Chela swung as hard as she could and knocked the gun out of Figgady's hand. It flew to the floor. "He'll kill our baby!" she screamed.

Figgady grabbed her by the back of the neck and slammed her into the wall. He broke her nose and knocked her out cold. He stood over her for a second, pissed.

Prentice clicked his tongue. "Dat's a damn shame. Oh well. Anyway, where dey at?"

Figgady mugged him. "How we finna do dis?"

Prentice laughed. "Nigga, you finna tell me what I need to know. When you do, you'll get your daughter back, and that'll be that. It's as simple as one, two, three."

Figgady wasn't with that rat shit. But no principle, nobody, or nothing was worth his daughter's life. He would do anything to save her. She was his everything. "Bruh, in California."

"Yeah, I know dat. Where in California?"

"Oakland," Figgady said, defeated.

Prentice smiled harder. He knew that Figgady was telling him the truth. "Yeah, you see, I know he in Oakland. But where, muthafucka? I need an address."

Figgady felt like he wanted to scream. He hated Prentice with every fiber of his being. "Bitch-ass nigga, I'm from Chicago. I don't know shit about Oakland, or where the fuck he staying. I told you what city he in, and that's all I know."

"Well, fuck nigga, you betta get to doing yo' research because until you get me his address, and everything I need, I'ma have yo' seed. You can't do shit about it. Now where the fuck is he staying?"

Figgady lowered his head. He was so angry that his vision was blurry. Getting hoed wasn't a part of his make-up. He felt weak. "Look, man, I'll find out. Let me do what I gotta do. In the meantime, let me see something that proves to me that my daughter is okay."

"I ain't showing you shit. You get me what the fuck I'm asking for, and you'll get her li'l ass back. Ain't nothing happening until then." He directed Figgady to have a seat on the couch.

Figgady remained standing. "Nigga, you think that it's sweet or somethin'? You thank you just 'bout to snatch my baby, and once you get what you want out of me dat all of dis shit is gon' be over and done with? Huh?"

Prentice yawned. "Shut the fuck up. You just like to hear yourself talk, don't you?" Prentice took a seat on the couch and crossed his legs. He rested his pistols on his lap.

Figgady couldn't believe the nuttiness of Prentice. He was acting like Figgady wasn't a killa. Figgady felt so disrespected that he thought about picking up his gun and airing Prentice out. His heart was pounding in his chest.

"You's a bitch nigga, Figgady. You act like you 'bout dat life, but you see, I take dat shit to a whole other level. I live dis shit. You just a bitch-ass nigga from Chicago."

Figgady stepped in front of him. "Yeah, dat's how you feel?"

Prentice laughed. "Wanna know how easy it is to make yo' ass bow down to me? Watch dis. Kneel, bitch nigga."

"Kneel? Nigga, fuck you. I'll never kneel to no man. Especially not - "

Boom! Boom!

Figgady felt his left kneecap explode. He buckled and fell on to his right one. He groaned in pain, holding it. Blood rushed through his fingers. "You bitch-ass nigga."

Chela opened her eyes and winced in pain. "Ohhh." She held her head. Her nose was broken.

Prentice stood up. "Look at you, nigga. You's a bitch. Prentice rushed Figgady and placed his gun to his neck. "Bitch nigga, if you don't get me what I want, I'ma make yo' life and all the lives of those you love a living hell. Find them! Or else." He smacked him as hard as he could with the pistol.

***

Mudman rolled his Benz with his arm around Keisha's shoulders. He looked over at her and approved her sexiness. "Damn, shawty, you looking good as a muthafucka tonight baby, no lie."

Keisha smiled. "I know. Everybody always hollering dat redbone shit, dey need to get a load of dis chocolate." She batted her eyelashes at him.

"Shawty, don't get yo' li'l ass whooped. Fuck you mean dey need to get a hold of dat chocolate? You thank 'cause I let you show Payroll yo' pussy dat ma'fuckas finna be able to go at my womb or somethin'?" he asked, looking down on her seriously.

"Nall, mane. Calm yo' crazy ass down. I was just fuckin' wit' you." She kissed his cheek. "Ain't no other nigga finna touch dis hurr pussy ever again. You already know dat shit right thurr."

"Dat's mo' like it." Mudman kept cruising. "Why you got dis li'l girl over our house, shawty?"

Keisha smiled devilishly. "She wanna be over here tonight. She say she wanna help me cook."

Mudman pulled the car up the driveway and parked behind Keisha's truck. He popped the trunk and grabbed the grocery bags. Before he could get them in his hands good enough, Savanna opened their front door. She was wearing a pair of tight-fitting booty shorts that were all in her crevice. From the distance that Mudman stood, he could make out her little camel toe.

"Girl, come down hurr and grab some of dese bags." Keisha ordered. She grabbed three of them and headed into the house.

Savanna came outside and grabbed two bags. She made her way to the house with Mudman walking behind her. Her ass cheeks jiggled with every step that she took on her pretty toes. Mudman couldn't take his eyes off of her booty. He was betting that her pussy was tight. Her mother made her stay in the house too much for it to have not been. She got up the stairs and looked back at him. "How was your day?"

He ignored her and kept looking at that young ass. "Take them in the house and set them on the table."

"Okay."

***

Later that night after they were done eating, Keisha turned on some dance music. She and Savanna danced in front of Mudman while he sat on the couch and watched them. Keisha pulled Savanna to her and squeezed all over her booty. She even yanked the shorts further into her crack.

Savanna moaned. "Mmm. Keisha, what are you doing?"

Keisha slid her fingers into her leg holes from the back. She played over her yellow sex lips. Mudman could see her pussy lips. The sight made his piece hard. Keisha sucked on the girl's neck.

"Rome, I want some of dis li'l bitch. But you already know I ain't finna do nothing without you. Let's take her li'l ass down." Keisha yanked her panties all the way to the side and exposed her naked slit. It was hairless and puffy. She slid a finger into her. "You like dat, bitch?"

"Mmm," Savanna moaned, spacing her feet. She looked over her shoulder at Mudman. "I ain't never did it before with a boy though."

Keisha gripped that ass. "It's all good. Come on."

She grabbed her hand and guided her into the bedroom. They fell on the bed with Keisha on top of Savanna. She pulled up her blouse and revealed her B-cups. The nipples were already erect. Keisha took to sucking the right one while Savanna moaned under her.

Mudman sat beside them. He looked between Savanna's thighs and saw how fat her li'l cat was. He leaned down and caught a whiff of her arousal. Then he was rubbing her coochie. It felt hot and meaty.

Savanna opened her thighs further for him. She hoped that she looked good down there. She didn't know what to expect, but everything that Keisha was doing was driving her crazy. She wanted more of it. She didn't think she could ever get enough.

Mudman slid his face between her thighs and started to eat her with expertise.

"Uhhhh! Man! Oooh! Yes!" She opened her thighs as far as she could and humped into his face.

Mudman held her by the fat ass cheeks and munched away. His tongue made circles around her clit. Then he was sucking on it hard. Two fingers slid in and out of her box at full speed.

Keisha pinched her nipples and pulled them. "Cum, li'l bitch. Cum on my nigga's tongue." She bit into her neck hard.

Savanna screamed and came hard, bucking and shaking. It seemed like as soon as it felt like it was going to go away, Mudman would suck harder on her clit and send her into another orgasm. She wrapped her thick thighs around his head and came again. She collapsed on the bed.

Keisha laid on the side of her and they French kissed loudly. Keisha held Savanna's pussy lips wide open for Mudman. "Hit that young pussy, baby. Break her li'l ass in."

Mudman didn't have to be told twice. He placed his big head on her wet opening and rubbed it up and down her slit. He cocked it back and slid into her furnace. Her pretty toes cringed. He got to fucking her at full speed, watching his dick go in and out of her.

"Unn! Unn! Unn! Mommy! Unn! Mmm! Shoot! Shoot. He so deep! Uhhhh!" Savanna hollered.

Keisha fingered herself watching Mudman tear Savanna off. It was a secret of Keisha's. She liked younger females. She couldn't contain herself around the real young bad ones. She'd been wanting to play with Savanna ever since she had laid eyes on the girl. Now that Mudman had joined in on the fun, it made it ten times better for her. She worked herself over and sucked on Savanna's perky nipples.

Mudman couldn't believe how tight her pussy was! He forced her right knee to her breasts and pounded as hard as he could. He felt her squeeze him, and then he was pulling out am cumming all over her stomach and breasts. "Arrgh! Shit! Shit!"

Savanna jumped up from the bed. She sat up and pumped his piece. She wanted it back in her. His fluids splashed her cheeks. "Please. Please. Put it back in. I need it."

Keisha pulled her to the bed and dived between her thighs. She started to eat her hungrily.

There was a loud pounding on the door. The trio broke apart. Keisha jumped up. Mudman put his dick up and pulled his pistol from the dresser. "Y'all stay in hurr." He rushed to the front door. He stopped and peeked out of the window. Sweat slid down the side of his face. He saw Sandra balancing her weight from one foot unto the next. She looked worried. "Keisha, its Sandra."

Keisha and Savanna scrambled to get dressed. They were moving all about the room, picking up discarded panties. Then Keisha was opening a window and spraying perfume to let out the scent of fucking. "Girl, hurry up, and go get in dat shower. We gon' finish yo' li'l young ass off tonight. I promise. I'ma get him hooked on that li'l pussy right hurr so we can fuck you whenever I want us to. You hurr me?" She pulled her to her and sucked all over her lips while she squeezed her plump ass.

"Yes."

Mudman moved so that Sandra could step into the house. She came inside and dropped her head. "Mudman, where is Keisha?"

Keisha stepped into the living room. She avoided eye contact with her. She felt slightly guilty for what she and

Mudman had been doing with her daughter. "Hurr I am right hurr. What's good?"

"Girl, I don't know how to tell you dis, but dey just found yo' mama dead in her house. I think somebody killed her."

Keisha felt like all of the air had been stripped from her lungs. She felt to her knees and held her chest. "Please, God, tell me dis ain't happening. Tell me dis ain't happening right now."

Chapter 15

It was five days later, two days before Kimmie's funeral. Mudman stood over Keisha as she sat at the dining room picking Mollie from the side of her hand. She savored the taste and swallowed the pink powder. She prayed for the euphoria that it was sure to give. After she finished her business, she sat back with a bottle of water in her hand. "I still can't believe my mama gone. She ain't never did nothing to nobody. First Kayla, and now hurr. Dis shit hurr ain't right, mane. It just ain't. Now you saying dat we can't even go down thurr because the Feds might be waiting to snatch is up? Mane, dis shit ain't right at all."

Mudman stood in silence. He was fucked up off of a couple drugs. The euphoria in his brain was minimal. He was trying to come to grips with the fact that his grandmother had reached out to him and told him that his mother had also been murdered in a similar like fashion to Keisha's. He knew they were being hunted. Whoever had done this to them was obviously trying to get back at either one or the both of them. Mudman was thinking Cartel. That made him angry. "Shawty, I'm telling you. As soon as we step foot in Louisiana, dem people gon' snatch our asses up and give us a whole lot of time. When they looking for a ma'fucka, that's usually how they smoke them out. By funerals, weddings, sweepstakes, or something along those lines."

"So, you saying dat the Feds did dis shit to my mama? They fucked her over like dis?" she asked, jumping up from the couch and balling up her fists.

"Nall, Shawty. Whoever did dis shit definitely in da life. Dey could be trying to clap at you, or me. Maybe both of us. I don't know. One thangs for sho' though, I'ma finna find out." He pulled her to him and wrapped her in his arms.

"I just wanna bury my mama, Rome. I wanna see her for da last time before dey put her in the ground. Why is dat asking too much?" She wanted to cry but refused to. Tears were no longer a part of her make up. Tears didn't solve anything, she thought. They only allowed for her to dwell on things. She didn't want to dwell. She wanted to mourn her mother in her heart and move on. She wished that she was stronger. "Rome, dey must not have had nothing against you if dey only fucked over my mother. I just don't understand. Who could have done dis?"

Mudman continued to rub her back. He kissed her forehead. "Baby, dey took a major shot at me too. You ain't in dis shit alone, trust me on dat."

"What do you mean?" Keisha looked up at him.

Mudman sighed and eased out of her embrace. "I just found out dat dey killed my mother too. My grandmother told me that they found her murdered in her house." He felt sick to his stomach. "Whoever did dis shit call myself clapping back at, like I said, either one, or the both of us."

Keisha eased from his embrace and looked into to his handsome dark skinned face. "When did you find dis out?"

"Last night."

"And when were you going to tell me, Rome? When?"

"When I was ready to. Dis ain't something that I want you dwelling on. I gotta get out here in those streets and find out who did dis shit." He tried to hug her.

Keisha pushed him away. "Nall, get off of me. We got so many fuckin' enemies. It could be anybody. Maybe it's one of Prentice's people that found out that we killed him and dis is their way of clapping back at us."

"It could be. Like I said, I'ma find out. Until I do, I want yo' ass to stay in dis house. Dem streets ain't safe out dere for you."

"You got me fucked up. I done lost my mother and my sister. You're the only person I got left in dis world. If you think I'm finna let you run dem streets while I sit in dis house like some wimp until you can figure things out, you got the game twisted. I'm coming wit' you. And I'm wit' whatever you wit'. Straight like dat."

Mudman looked her over. He didn't feel like arguing with her. He knew that the more Keisha hung around him, the more she became just like him. She wasn't going to take no for an answer. "A'ight, shawty, check dis out. I thank it's the Cartel."

"Which one? It's so many of dem ma'fuckas back home and out hurr. How you gon' know which one to go at?"

"Nall, I ain't talking 'bout none of dem dope boy-ass cartels. I'm talking 'bout dat one dat's down dere in Mexico. Dem real ma'fuckas."

Keisha's eyes got bucked. "Da Sinaloa one?"

Mudman nodded. "Or it could be dem Dominicans out of Lawrence, over dere in Boston. I gotta reach out to a few of my potnas back dat way and see what's really good. In the meantime, I gotta handle some local bidness. Mars got the low down on one of the headquarters for dem boys out of Cypress Village. He already got a couple bitches inside, and a few of his niggas from J Crew that's ready to break away from the Cypress. I promised them dat with me in power that their crews would make more money den dey do now. You already know how dey run shit out hurr in Oakland. It's all about da money. So, we finna go over hurr and see if dis ma'fucka will step down easily, or of its gon' take some convincing. Either way, I'ma get my answer tonight."

Keisha nodded her head as the Mollie kicked in. She got a sudden strong blast of euphoria. Her pupils dilated. She felt calmer. She could now think straight. "Look, I don't give a fuck what you thank you 'bout to do. Either way, I'm coming wit' you. From now, on we shed blood together." She walked up to him and slid her arms around his waist.

Mudman allowed for her to do that. Then he grabbed her by the throat with both hands and squeezed. He could feel her choking. Her eyes got big. She smacked at his hands. He pushed her back into the wall and kept choking. She struggled against him. In an instant, he let her go. She took in a gasp of air. He kissed her lips, and tongued her down, squeezing, and rubbing all over her ass. "We die together, Keisha. Me and you, bae. Me and you."

Keisha had already cum while he choked her. She jumped up on him and wrapped her thighs around his waist. She bit his lip. "I love you, Rome. I love you so much. I'll die for you. I swear to God I will."

Mudman held her up and moved her panties to the side under her skirt. He released himself and slid into her depths, slamming her down on his pole over and over again. She gripped him and groaned into his ear. Get it out yo' system, baby. She gone. She gone, boo."

Tears spilled out of Keisha's eyes as he bounced her up and down. He fucked her faster and faster. Her ankles locked around his waist. He reached deeper and deeper into her womb. "Uhhhh!" The Mollie took over and caused her to cum hard. She screamed into his ear again.

Mudman was in a frenzy. Keisha was so wet that it felt like she was peeing on him. He fucked faster. He held her ass and put it down. "No love. No love. Black hearts. Black hearts. Me and you. Us. Shit! Us!" He slammed her down as hard as he could and came inside of her.

They fell to the carpet. Keisha jumped on top of him and put his piece back inside herself. She rested her hands on his bulletproof vest and rode him fast with her head tilted backward. Her knees scraped against the carpet. It added to her pleasure in a weird way. She bit into his neck and came.

Mudman felt her shivering on him. He gripped her big ass and continued to slam her down hard. He wanted to make sure that she was taking all of his piece, and she was. When she spun all the way around with his dick still inside of her, he nearly came again. She held his ankles and bounced harder. He watched her pussy swallow him hungrily. The sight became too much. He came again, smacking her on the ass.

Keisha arched her back with tears running down her cheeks and came as hard as she ever had. She released the pains from the loss of her sister and mother through their act. She felt weaker, yet stronger at the same time. She could hear the chanting of his black heart mantra inside of her mind. She knew that if she was going to roll beside Mudman on a daily basis, her heart had to become as black as his.

***

"So, this what it is. Y'all gon' stay on yo' side of this here district and leave Cypress Village out everything you got going on. Dis is my turf. I run dis shit. My father ran it before me, and his before him. It's my birthright. You got Acorn Projects, and the City Towers. That's cool. But it's gon' be a cold day in hell before you take over Cypress Village," Forty said, sitting back, and holding an AK47 up against his shoulder to make a display. He had four killas standing behind him and others stationed around the dungeon, armed and ready for war. He wanted Mudman to know that he meant bidness.

Mudman didn't like the rank smell of the dungeon they were in. It felt hot. It smelled bad, and he didn't quite remember how they had gotten into the underground dungeon that they were in. He remembered traveling down to the subway and jumping on the tracks. Once they went behind a wall and took a flight of stairs that led to a maze like path below Cypress Village, he lost the compass in his head.

Mars sat beside Mudman. He eyed Forty with hatred. He knew the man wasn't tough. He'd whooped his ass enough times growing up to have proved that. His position was, like he said, handed down. It was given, not earned. If it was up to him, he would have splashed Forty and smoked his entire crew of eighty with no remorse.

"Da way I see it, Forty, you ain't got no muthafuckin' choice. Acorn is reestablishing itself, and the only ma'fucka standing in da way of dat is you. You got Cypress Village. You could either merge with us and fall under me, or we gon' be forced to smash you dead. It's simple as dat.

Forty laughed. He looked to Mudman, then to Mars and over to Keisha. She had a serious mug on her face that tickled him. He wondered what kind of leader brought a bitch along for the ride. He didn't know how they did business in the south, but this was Oakland. His homeland. His turf. He was dead set on protecting it with everything that he had as a man.

"Say, homie, I don't know what you think this is, but ain't none of dat bout to happen with Cypress Village, homie. We got a system around dis ma'fucka, a system that you gon' follow. Now I ain't tryna stop you from doing what you do over there but keep that shit over there. You ain't got no win in my section."

Mudman nodded. "You sho' 'bout dat?"

Forty cocked his AK. "Oh, I'm damn sho'."

Mudman scanned the dungeon. He saw four men to his left that were a part of Forty's detail. Then his eyes scanned to the right. He saw four more. Behind Forty were two other armed hittas. He could smell the scent of Keisha's perfume. It reminded him that he had to protect her at all costs. He wanted to send things up with Forty right then and there, but he had to be smart. He nodded. "Well, a'ight den. I guess we gon' agree that we both disagree. It's all good. Let's roll, fellas." Mudman stood and pushed out his chair.

Forty stood as well. "It's a shame that we come to some form of an agreement. Best I can tell you is to stay on yo' side of the hood, and I'll stay on mine."

Mudman smiled and kept walking. "A'ight, potna."

Mars stepped past Forty and looked him in the eyes. He couldn't stand the man. He hated the sight of him. He also hated being in his presence.

Keisha was the last to get up and follow her homies toward the door of the dungeon. She was two steps away from Mudman when Forty grabbed her ass and squeezed it. "Damn, Mudman, dis li'l bitch thick right here. Where da fuck you find her at?"

Keisha didn't hesitate. She upped a .44, placed it to Forty's left eye, and pulled the trigger two quick times.

Forty saw the bright fire and felt the left side of his face rip off. He dropped his AK and fell in what seemed like slow motion. Before he hit the ground, everything went black. He was deceased.

Keisha got to bucking down Forty's crew. Mudman joined in on the gun fight, stepping beside her. Then Mars and the rest of their troops were firing. They caught the men off guard. It sounded like a war movie in the dungeon. Mudman pulled Keisha backward while they continued to fire over and over.

Keisha held her tongue out of her mouth. She popped her pistol back to back. The smell of the gun powder, the feel of the kick of her guns… All of it caused pussy juice to run down her thighs into her jeans. She busted at every enemy moving. She watched her bullets enter into their bodies, dropping them.

Mars let his Draco spit rapidly. "Let's go! Hurry up!"

Mudman forced Keisha out of the dungeon. He and Mars stood side by side and aired out Forty's crew. The majority of the men took off running after firing a few slugs. The ones that stayed to return fire wound up slumped, especially after a few that they thought were with them turned on them and started to fire at then as well. Mars had set enemies among so-called friends. The massacre had worked out in their favor.

Chapter 16

Chela sat in front of Figgady with her hair all over the place. She hugged herself and rocked back, and forth. She was sick. The heroin was calling her. She didn't know what to do. She watched him shoot the drug into his veins. It felt like she was being tortured. When he pulled it out and moaned, she thought she was going to scream.

Figgady felt the effects of the drug right away. He nodded his head forward, slept for three seconds, and placed the syringe on the table. He leaned back and opened his eyes.

Chela was knelt on the floor in front of him. Tears ran down her cheeks. "I need it."

Figgady eyed her through hazy eyes. "You need what?"

She held up his syringe and wiped her nose. Her stomach was turned in knots. She kept farting. She was seconds away from releasing her bowels. She couldn't control what her body was doing.

Figgady ran his hand over his face. "Fuck you talking 'bout shawty? You don't fuck wit' dis shit. Since when?"

Chela grabbed the syringe and licked the tip of it. She tasted his blood with a hint of the Tar. It made her shiver. She farted some more and began to shake uncontrollably. "Figgady give me some! Fix my shit right now! Please!"

"What? Bitch, I ain't giving you none of this shit. It's a death sentence." He stood up and buckled slightly. Prentice had knocked off his knee cap. He could barely move around without groaning and being in intense, excruciating pain.

She slowly came to her feet. She turned her hands into fists. "If you don't give me what I want, I swear to God you finna have to kill me. Now I need some of that dope. I'm gon' get it, one way or the other."

"Bitch, please." He yanked his syringe out of her hand and muffed her to the floor.

Chela covered her face and screamed into her hands. When she removed them, she saw Figgady flicking a four and a half ounce package of Sinaloa with his finger. She jumped up and ran into the kitchen. She grabbed a butcher's knife and came back into the living room. "Gimme what I want, Figgady. She farted. Gravy-like shit oozed out of her back door. She ignored the heat as it traveled down the back of her thigh. Her ass cheeks felt soupy.

Figgady saw that she had a knife in her hand. He frowned and faced her. "Bitch, don't play wit' me. Take yo' ass in there and sit down." He pointed toward the front room.

Chela felt like her insides were being ripped out of her. She farted again. More of the feces oozed out. She stepped forward. "Figgady, I need the dope. Please don't make me use this knife. I love you, but I need it so bad. I can't control myself."

Figgady pointed again. "Bitch, go in there, and sit yo' ass down. You not getting none of this dope. Fuck is wrong wit' you anyway? My daughter's mother ain't finna be no hype. Never."

She screamed and rushed him at full speed. When she got close enough, she slammed the knife into his shoulder and snatched the dope out of his hand. She took off running toward the back of the house.

Figgady hollered. He pulled the knife out immediately. He fell against the wall. It took him a second to regain his composure. He couldn't believe that his baby mother had stabbed him and taken his dope. Blood gushed through his fingers. He gritted his teeth. "Bitch, I'm finna kill you!" he roared.

Chela opened the back door and took off running down the alley barefoot at full speed. She dared not look back. When she got to the end of the alley, she ran across the street. She ran along side of a gangway, hopped the fence, and ran out of that backyard. She kept running and running. She ran until she had to stop. She wound up under somebody's back porch. As soon as she could, she took a pinch of the dope and tooted it up her nose. She shivered and did it again. She needed a syringe bad. She craved one. But for now, the tooting would have to do.

Figgady limped out of the house and into the backyard. "Chela! Chela! Shay-LA!" he hollered.

But Chela was long gone, and in another world.

***

Prentice took the three big master locks off of the door and pulled open the creaky wooden door. He stepped into the room that was being used to hold Chiah prisoner. Prentice took the wrappings off of the McDonald's cheeseburger and tossed it on the floor in front of Chiah. "Here you go, li'l girl. Eat up."

Chiah looked up at him with her big almond eyes. They were red from crying. "No thank you. I'm not hungry. I just want my mama and daddy," she whined.

Prentice snickered. "Shawty, you ain't finna get neither one of dem. You might as well eat dat damn fool. Come on now. He kicked it closer to her.

"I said I'm not hungry. Now leave me alone and go get my parents. You bully." She frowned her face and crossed her arms in front of her chest. She had lost five pounds since she'd been in the Ninth Ward basement. Prentice thought it was a good idea to keep her in New Orleans' Ninth Ward because the police presence was so minimal. After Hurricane Katrina twelve years prior, it was like the area had been forgotten about. That worked in his favor.

Prentice picked up the cheeseburger, grabbed Chiah by the hair, and stuffed the burger into her face. He kept mashing it until portions of it went inside of her mouth. She fought him. He slung her to the ground and kicked the remnants of the food into her chest. "Eat up, or I'ma kill you," he threatened.

Chiah cried hard. She picked up the food and started to eat it, though her stomach constantly turned. "I hate you, Prentice. You're a mean bully!"

Prentice stood over her. "Bitch, eat dat food. You getting too fucking skinny. You ain't finna die on my watch. Only way you die is if I kill you." He knelt down and began stuffing the food into her mouth.

Chiah chewed. She choked. She swallowed. She fought at him. He allowed for her to breathe only a few seconds before he was stuffing her face with food again. After the burger was complete, he handed her a juice.

"Drink it up."

She cried and followed his orders. "I hate you. When my dad finds me, he's going to kill you."

Prentice laughed. "You thank yo' daddy gon' kill me, huh?"

She nodded. "I know he is. He loves me so much."

Prentice stared at her for a long time. He looked into her dirty, yet pretty face, and smiled. He smacked the juice from her hand and grabbed her by the thin T-shirt he had her wearing. "Now you listen to me, you li'l bitch. Yo' daddy can't fuck wit' my bidness."

"Let me go!" she cried.

"Only reason he or yo' mama still got breath in dey lungs is because I need them. If I didn't, I'da smoked both of dem, and you." He threw her to the ground.

She curled into a ball. "I just wanna get out of here. Please just let me go home. I'm begging you."

Prentice stood up. He watched her squirm on the floor. She looked helpless. The shirt barely covered her frame. It was so thin that she was shivering. He shook his head. "Get up!"

She ignored him. "I wanna go home. I hate it here."

"I said get up!" He yanked her by the shirt and wound up ripping it off of her. He grabbed her by the throat and held her naked against the wall. "You hate me? Huh? You hate me?" He squeezed tighter.

She kicked her legs out at him. She wrapped them around his bulging bicep and smacked at his hand. She couldn't breathe. Her system began to panic. She started to pee.

Prentice held her with two hands now. "You hate me? Huh? Yeah? Well, I hate Keisha! Dat bitch played me. All you hoes alike. All of you. Young, old. Don't matter. It don't matter. Who you gon' hurt, huh? Who?" He started laughing and squeezing harder. "Aw yeah, nobody. Not a muthafuckin' soul. He squeezed as hard as he could and crushed her throat.

Chiah felt her throat cave inward. It was the worst pain she had ever felt before. She closed her eyes as her lungs burst. Her insides filled up with blood. Seconds later, she was dead.

Prentice kept choking. He held her up as high as he could, shaking her. After she went slack in his hands, he looked up at her. He sniffed her all over. The scent of her drove him crazy. He slung her against the wall as hard as he could, imagining that she was Keisha. She fell to the ground, unmoving.

Suddenly, the psychotic haze left him. He looked down on Chiah with new eyes. Prentice held his head with two hands. "What have I done? What have I done?" He rushed to Chiah and picked her up. He laid his cheek against hers. "Shit, I'm so sorry, shawty. I just hate Keisha so much. I hate you,

Keisha! I hate you!" He stood up and began to stomp Chiah over and over for five full minutes imagining that she was Keisha.

***

Later that night, Prentice sat across from Figgady at Rose's Barbecue. He sucked the spicy barbecue sauce from his fingers loudly. He looked over to Figgady and smiled. "Chela was using dat shit when she came to me. I just gave her some of my product after she asked for it," he lied, looking Figgady directly in the eyes. "Did you get what I asked you for?"

Figgady nodded and reluctantly slid the Oakland address across the table to him. "Dis where he laying his head right now. I'm supposed to fly out there to meet him in a few days. He finishing up some last minute bidness first."

Prentice picked up the address and studied of carefully. "What da fuck dis nigga doing staying in Acorn? I'm surprised dem killas out dey way ain't knocked his head off of his shoulders yet." He folded up the piece of paper and tucked it into his shirt pocket.

Figgady sat there patiently for a few moments. Then he got irritated as Prentice continued to eat his baby back ribs with no regard for the second half of their dealings. "A'ight, nigga, you got what the fuck you wanted. Now whurr is my shawty at?"

Prentice kept eating. He poured hot sauce on top of his ribs, then added more of the patented barbecue sauce that Rose invented. "Fuck is you so impatient for? Don't you know that I gotta confirm all dis shit before I do anythang else?" He laughed. "Nigga, you know how dis shit hurr go."

Figgady jumped up in the dimly-lit restaurant. "You stupid muthafucka, a deal is a deal. Where da fuck is my baby? I'm tired of playing dese games with you."

Prentice continued to eat his food. He got a piece of meat stuck in his tooth and stopped to pick at it. He used the fork. He used a piece of folded paper. Finally, he was able to remove it with a toothpick. He blew the trapped meat across the restaurant. He took a sip of his pink lemonade that he'd poured two tablets of Mollie into and sat back. "Figgady, kiss my ass, nigga. Dat lil girl straight. She getting better treatment than Kylie Jenner right now," he lied. "When I can confirm that all of dis checks out, you can get Princess back. But for now, I need you to set up a meeting with Mudman. Tell him you coming to Oakland. Once he set up a time and date for you to arrive, I will give you the address and place sure Chiah is. At the same time, you embrace her, I'll be doing what I gotta do with him. The sooner the better." He took a long swallow from his lemonade.

Figgady sat there steaming. He was ready to pop off. Sweat poured down the back of his neck. It slid to his waistband. He eyed Prentice with a murderous glare. "You bitch-ass nigga. You thank I'm sweet."

"As a sugar cane," Prentice retorted. "Now sit yo' pussy ass down, before I make you menstruate."

Figgady was shaking like crazy. He slowly sat down and tried to keep Chiah at the forefront of his brain. "A'ight, Prentice, but dis da last thang I'm doing for yo' monkey ass. If one hair has been harmed on my daughter, nigga, on my soul, you gon' get - "

Prentice reached across the table and pulled Figgady forward by his dreads. He pressed his Glock to the side of his neck and cocked the hammer. "Bitch nigga, it ain't in yo' best interest to keep on threatening me. You don't want dese problems. And you ain't 'bout dat life." He dumped the jar of sugar that he was using to sweeten his lemonade to his liking on top of Figgady's head. "You sweet as bear meat, boy." He pushed him backwards and tucked his gun.

Figgady landed against the back of the booth. He felt like a bitch. He vowed that as soon as he got his daughter back, he was going to kill Prentice. He felt so adamant about that that he would have literally killed anybody who smoked Prentice first. He jumped up. "I'm finna handle my bidness. Have my daughter ready to go."

Prentice sat back and kicked his feet up. He was operating on a whole other murderous level. He wasn't worried about nothing or nobody. If it came down to it, he was ready to die. Nothing but death could keep him from bodying both Keisha and Mudman. The thought of murdering them had become an addiction for him. It was all he could think about. "The sooner the better," he grumbled. He mugged Figgady as he and his crew filed out to their cars and pulled away from the restaurant. As soon as he confirmed Keisha and Mudman's locations, he would finish Figgady and Chela off as well. "Why not?" he hissed.

Chapter 17

"I gotta say, Mudman, I am impressed. You said that if I gave you some time that you would surely conquer The City Towers, Cypress Village, and Acorn Projects. Well, my man, if I am being told the right information, it seems to me that you are the man. There is really nobody standing in place to challenge you. Well, that is, until Nike gets home in a few months. You betta believe that when he gets home that he's coming for the crown. I'm willing to bet the house on that," Miguelito said, as he handed Mudman the bottle of pure codeine.

Mudman didn't drink behind no man. He thought that was a little too weird, and gross. He pushed the bottle away from him. "I'm straight Wardy. I'm already leaning like a ma'fucka. And as far as Nike go, I'll worry about him when it's time too. For now, I'm ready to sit down and meet The Bull."

The Bull was the head of the Bloodthirsty Cartel. He was given the slot to stand over the state of California, amongst a few others, but Mudman didn't care about them. He only cared about California because that's the state that he was operating out of.

Miguelito rolled his Porsche in silence. He turned down the Reggaeton music and rubbed at his chin hairs. One glance into his rearview mirror told him that his security team was following at a safe distance. He also had a car in the front of his Porsche that was heavily armed. Each car had expensive high frequency scanners and police detectors. "You know how many muthafuckas actually get to meet the Bull and live to tell about it?" he asked.

"Nope. But I plan on being one of the ma'fuckas dat do." Mudman popped a stick of Winterfresh gum into his mouth and chewed.

Miguelito laughed at that. "The Bull wants to meet you because he's heard a lot about you. Not only about the shit you've done in Oakland, but your name rings bells in Louisiana as well. He says that you were the cause of many disruptions to his operations." Miguelito looked over at Mudman.

"I probably was. If ma'fuckas was eating around me in Baton Rouge, and I wasn't able to eat off da plate wit' dem, I took a good look at 'em."

"What would you say of you found out that many of the people you hit down there were linked into the Bull and the Bloodthirsty Cartel?"

Mudman shrugged his shoulders. "I wouldn't give no fuck. It is what it is. I played a different game back den. I was a stick up kid to the max. I didn't give a fuck who the niggas I hit were connected to. All of dis shit is a part of the same dirty-ass game. Dope boys and jack boys. It all comes with the territory. The Bull wanna come at me over dat den, man... Bring it on." Mudman popped two Percocets and chewed them.

Miguelito felt from then on that Mudman must have been lacking good sense. He didn't have any idea if he was being led, or he did, and to Miguelito it seemed like it didn't matter to him. He was either very dumb or fearless, Miguelito guessed. He needed to feel him out some more to get a better read.

"Okay, Mudman, let me just ask you a question. Do you have any idea what The Bull could do to you?"

"Da same thangs he could do to me, I could do to him. I ain't really worried 'bout it. My death date already set in stone." He leaned his seat back and checked his phone. He had a few messages from Figgady. He knew he had to get up with him so he could figure out when he was going to link up with him out in Oakland. Figgady had texted that he was over visiting his grandparents in San Francisco. That was only a short drive away. "Anyway, what's going to be expected of me when we get here?"

"Respect. You are going to approach The Bull with the utmost respect. If you want him to give you his blessing of business, then it starts with this sit down. Keep in mind that he very rarely sits down with any of his potential associates. You should treat this meeting as sacred."

Mudman didn't know about all that. He knew he needed the plug, but it wasn't in him to kiss anybody's ass. He would play his role accordingly and take things from there. "A'ight, bruh, I got you."

Miguelito turned on to a dirt road and slowed his car down. The speed limit was seventy-five, and he was only traveling fifty. Mudman looked at the speedometer and gave him a crazy look. "What's the matter?" Miguelito asked.

"Fuck you going so slow for?" Mudman asked. A big eighteen wheeler sped in front of them. "Even dis ma'fucka passing us up."

Miguelito slowed his Porsche even more. "Chill, homes."

"Chill? Fuck dat's supposed to mean?"

The back doors to the eighteen wheeler opened up. Two armed guards lowered a ramp while three more stood by on security. The ramp slowly lowered to the road until it was causing sparks to fly from the highway. Miguelito maneuvered the Porsche and rolled up on the ramp. He eased up and into the back of the truck. As soon as he was all the way inside, the guards closed the back to the semi-truck.

Miguelito cut the headlights and turned off the ignition and dashboard lights.

Mudman sat in darkness. He caught on right away. He remained silent and allowed for his eyes to adjust to the bitter darkness. They tuned in only slightly. He still couldn't see where any of the men had gone. He wished that Miguelito would have kept on the lights.

"Dis all a part of the process, Mudman. Yo' best bet is to lean back and chill. We finna be in darkness for a few hours," Miguelito said.

Mudman nodded and fell back. Four text messages came through from Figgady in a row. Mudman didn't like no nigga sweating him, especially if he was hitting him up more than Keisha was. That was weird to him and sent his suspicions on high alert. He would have to pick Figgady's brain when his mission was over. It's the only thing that made sense.

***

Four hours later, Mudman, sat in a hard metal chair next to Miguelito inside of a cave in Arizona. He didn't know where he was or when The Bull would show up, but he was becoming restless. The cave smelled like bat shit. It was extremely humid, and all kinds of bugs were crawling all over him and biting him periodically. He was irritated, and he wanted to snap out so bad, but he knew that it would have cost him his life.

The cave was illuminated by the headlights from the four wheelers that had used to travel into the cave with. He could feel his Kevlar vest sticking to him, and he had to piss worse than he ever had before. He moved only slightly, and the armed gunmen moved in on him and aimed their assault rifles at him. Mudman looked past them as if he didn't see them. He knew not to make any more sudden moves.

Miguelito felt a trickle of sweat bubble up on his forehead and slide down the side of his face. It slid along the side of his sideburns and felt like a bug, but he refused to wipe it away. He knew better. One forced move, and the shooters for the Bloodthirsty Cartel would take his life.

There was the sound of wheels crunching gravel. The shooters perked up and took their weapons off of Mudman. They rushed to the entrance of the cave and aimed their assault rifles. Four of them held grenades ready to blow yo anybody that came through the cave that wasn't authorized to do so. Bats screeched overhead. The men scrambled as their walkie talkies sounded. It alerted them and let them know that The Bull was there, that everybody needed to be on point.

Mudman sat still. He looked toward the entrance and felt a sigh of relief as The Bull came riding into the dungeon on an all-black four wheeler. He was trailed by three armed bodyguards on four wheelers, and two in front of him that were equally armed.

The Bull rolled his ATV and jumped off of it. He stood 5'3" inches tall. He weighed 160 pounds. He had a bushy mustache under his nose and wore tight Levi jeans with a big gold belt buckle. He wore a cowboy hat and boots. He stepped in front of Mudman and looked down on him. "Dis da deadly son of a bitch they been telling me about?" he asked in Spanish.

Miguelito nodded and looked back at the ground. "Yes, Bull."

The Bull squat down and looked into Mudman's grill. "Do you know who I am?"

Mudman looked into his brown eyes and nodded. "Yep, I sho' do."

The Bull continued to glare at him. "You caused me a lot of problems back in Baton Rouge. A lot of problems, and a lot of money. What you gotta say about that?"

Mudman shrugged his shoulders. "I eat to live, and I live to eat."

"What?" The Bull was confused. He wasn't sure if he heard him correctly.

"I said I eat to live, and I live to eat. Bitch niggas, dat is. I don't give a fuck about dem cartels I slumped back home. I don't give a fuck about da ones I slumped here because I live to eat. If a ma'fucka operation look sweet enough to eat to me, I'm putting a napkin around my neck and I'm eating them. I don't give a fuck who day belong to."

The Bull's troops closed in on Mudman. They cocked their guns and aimed them at him again. The Bull continued to squat, trying to figure Mudman out. "Do you have any idea what I can do to you right now?"

"You can make me a rich man. Dat's what you can do. Dat's all I want. I wanna be well da fuck off. I wanna be able to spoil my shawty and live good. I been struggling in da slums my whole life. Shit been real bad for a long time, but I ain't complaining. You know why? Because I'ma get what I'm after whether you give it to me or not. Ain't nobody finna eat more den me in those streets. Ain't no cartel finna succeed without me crushing it. The game belongs to me. Dat's just how I feel. Nothing but death can keep me from it. Know dat."

The Bull stood up and pulled a machete from his sheath. Two big guards rushed to hold Mudman's shoulders. Mudman didn't even waste his time fighting against the binds. He sat still while The Bull placed the blade to his throat. "You know, there is somethin very Looney about you that I like. There is a reason why I didn't kill you back in Louisiana," he said, walking around Mudman.

"Yeah? Why is dat?"

The Bull grabbed his dreads and placed the blade against his Adam's apple. "Because you owe me a lot of money, number one. Number two, I see the king in you. You live the game. I feel like with a little push you could make me millions of dollars. Maybe even more than that. What you got to say about that?"

"I thank you right 'bout me making US a lot of money. Far as me owing you any thang, dat's yo' interpretation, not mine."

"Mine is the only one that counts." He snickered. "I'm willing to make you an offer. More like a proposition. You care to hear it?"

Mudman stayed still. "Yeah."

"Oakland, Los Angeles, and San Francisco can be yours - under me, of course - if you keep that same lethal attitude, and continue to crush all rivals in your community. I want the things that I supply you with to fully dominate the Black's and even the Latinos in California. You won't be alone, of course, but your job will be most important in your community. You do this and you can start to living the way you have always dreamed in a matter of years."

Mudman swallowed. He could feel the blade scrape against his Adam's apple. That pissed him off. "Sounds like a plan to me. When do we start?"

"Immediately." He took the blade away from his neck and stood back. "You have my hand. You will be given a quota to meet every two weeks. I will never take any excuses for what you owe me. You're short once, your life is mine. Yours, and all of those you love. Do you understand that?"

Mudman nodded. "When is the first shipment?"

The Bull mugged him for a long time. Then he busted up laughing. He tossed his head back and busted a gut. He didn't think Mudman had any idea what he was getting himself into.

Chapter 18

Mudman got his first shipment two weeks later and shut down the city. A week prior to his shipments, he'd issued out a decree that any dope boys caught serving around Cypress Village, Acorn Projects, or the City Towers that didn't have his stamp of approval would be smoked immediately. He flooded the streets with ruthless, coldhearted hittas that answered directly to him. They were given the order of no mercy. They didn't care if they saw car seats in the back of cars, they still chopped them down on sight if the dope boy inside looked as if he was answering his phone to complete a sale.

Mudman hit the ground running as well. He kicked in doors and let his hammers clack. The blood began to excite him more and more. With every kill, he felt himself becoming more implanted within the game. His name began to ring like crazy, so much so that those in Oakland began to look at him as a god in just a time span of three months. Though it was from mostly fear, Mudman ceased it just the same. In six short months, he'd taken over his portion of Oakland and began to spill over his operations into both the Latino and Asian sides of the city. Entering onto their turfs brought more him wars that Mudman could have ever imagined. It seemed to him that he was losing four to five hittas with every gunfight that he took part in. It was like he couldn't recruit more savage hearted shooters fast enough. Yet and still, there was no fold or buckle in Mudman. He set up recruiting posts inside of the Acorn Projects. Any young soldier that was down to pop that iron and ready to die beside him was given a slot inside of his cartel. As long as they pledged their allegiance to him, he took care of their families and made sure the shooter was paid no less than two thousand dollars every week. He supplied them with used cars that they in turn hooked up to look like something flashy. Mudman didn't care about the cars or the flash. For him, it was all about supremacy. He wanted to be a king, a legend, and he was well on his way to being exactly that. He knew that the road would continue to be paved in blood. He had no other choice than to own it.

***

In the seventh month after Mudman had fully taken over the slums, Payroll was sentenced to three years in prison for an old case that he had not told anyone about. A year before Mudman and Keisha had come to Oakland, he'd caught a battery to a female Postal Service worker. He'd been hopped up on PCP, out of his mind, and he'd beaten the woman pretty severely. Eighteen months later, he was being sentenced to three years in prison. Mudman visited him three weeks after he was sent upstate.

Payroll came into the visiting room with his prison tans on. He stopped mid-stride when he saw that both Keisha, and Mudman were sitting at the visiting room table. He felt a sense of anger and irritation. He walked into their vicinity and stopped in front of Keisha. "What up, cuz?"

Keisha stood up. She knew she had to play her role. Even though she didn't like Payroll because she felt that he was a pussy of a man, she had to stay focused. Mudman continued to remind her of that. She stepped into Payroll's open arms and hugged him. "Hey, cuz, how you holding up?"

Payroll sniffed her and felt his piece twinge. He looked into Mudman's gray eyes and closed his own. He wanted to enjoy hugging Keisha. She was so strapped, and soft. "I'm fucked up in here. Dis three years was a blind side. Luckily for me, dis shit day for day." He broke their embrace and took a seat across from them. He nodded to Mudman.

Mudman bowed his head once and imagined chopping Payroll's body into small pieces. "Why you ain't tell no ma'fucka about dis case right hurr, homeboy?"

Payroll shrugged his shoulders. "I forgot about dis shit, to be honest wit' you. It was so much other shit going on that dis case didn't even dawn on me, but I decided to hit up Justin Bivens.. He said he was gon' help me get a sentence modification a few months down the line wit' it. For now, he solely focused on Cartier's homie."

"As he should be. Dat ma'fucka ain't cheap. But every thang sound good doe," Mudman relayed.

"Yeah?" Payroll leaned in, anxious to know what Mudman had learned. "How so?"

"You know I don't know too much bout dat legal shit and thangs. Justin just say you got a good chance at beating da case 'cause you was shot up in the process, and it could be looked at as self-defense. Plus, dey never found da gun dat was used. You got a lot of shit dat's working in your favor. You should be out of hurr in no time."

"Dat's what's good. I go back down to the county next week fo' some child support shit. One of my old hoes got me jammed up. Hopefully we'll know something by den." He looked over the table that they had filled with all kinds of vending machine food. He picked up a double cheeseburger and started to put condiments on it. "Yeah, ma'fuckas been telling me how you done took over Oakland, Mudman. Dey say you been bussing heads left and right. You already know who you owe all dat success too."

"Yeah, nigga, me," Mudman retorted.

"You?" Payroll took a big bite off of his sandwich and started to chew of with his mouth open. "Shid, nigga, when you came out West, ain't nobody know who yo' country bumpkin ass was. Once you came up under me, ma'fuckas gave you yo' respect. Dey formed around you 'cause I told 'em to. I can break all dat shit up at any time. Trust those words, my nigga."

"Oh yeah?" Mudman slid to the edge of his seat.

"Yeah, homeboy." Payroll swallowed his food and eyed Mudman with anger. He nodded his head and sucked his fingers, then laughed. "I'ma need y'all to get shit moving a li'l faster than it's going. I'm starting to get restless. Now dat you making all dis money - money dat's supposed to be mine - I'ma need you to hit Justin Bivens with some more cash. Plus, I got some other licks I need you to hit for me. Only thang is- when you hit these few traps, I need for eighty percent of the money to come to me. You can do what you do on the one side, then on the other, I need my profits increased. You understand what I'm telling you?"

Mudman was seconds away from jumping out of his seat and crashing Payroll out. He felt his temper boiling. He wanted to fuck him over right then and there, but he had to be smart. To have snapped out on Payroll would have caused too much controversy within the crew of killas that he was forming. While he was the sole person taking care of the young hittas in his crew, a lot of them still looked up to Payroll for whatever reason, and they honored him as a god as well.

"Say, Payroll, maybe there I'd a more respectful way that you could come at us. Right now, you sounding rude as fuck. I don't know how Mudman feeling right now, but I for damn sho' ain't liking how you coming at us right now," Keisha said, getting irritated. She could sense that Mudman was seconds away from blowing up. She thought that it would be smarter for her to say something first before Mudman did. She sensed that he would speak with his fists instead of his words.

"I don't give a fuck how you or dis nigga feeling. Bitch, you killed Cartier. You pumped dat nigga full of slugs. Yet I'm the ma'fucka dat's sitting in here like a damn fool while y'all live da good life. Fuck I look like? A goof or somethin?"

Mudman fidgeted in his chair. He was trying his best to keep his composure. Now that he had The Bull backing his endeavors, he needed to be smart. He now had a quota to meet each month. If he failed to meet that quota, it was a death sentence for him and Keisha. That was a lot of pressure. It meant that everything had to be handled from a strategic standpoint. He forced a smile. "You know what, Payroll? You're right."

Keisha almost snapped her neck she turned it so fast to look at Mudman. "He is?"

"Yeah, shawty. We wouldn't have none of dis shit of it wasn't for Payroll."

"We wouldn't?" Now she was confused.

"N'all. Bruh da one plugged me into Oakland. He gave me the key to Coke Land." Coke Land was the nick name for Oakland. "Had he not done dat, we would still be pulling li'l meaningless kick doors."

Payroll cheesed proudly. "Don't forget I put you in with Miguelito too. Had you not got that plug, you wouldn't be fuckin wit' the Cartel right now either."

Mudman eyed him. He was caught off guard. "How da fuck you know 'bout any of dat shit thurr?"

"Just 'cause I'm in here don't mean I don't keep my ear to da street. I'm clocking yo' every move. Why? Because you sitting in my slot right now." He slammed his double cheeseburger to the table and slid to the front of his chair. "Check dis shit out, bitch-ass nigga. You too, bitch." He mugged Keisha. "I don't give a fuck about neither one of you two muthafuckas. Mudman, I'll smoke you. Keisha, after I fuck yo' li'l thick ass, cousin or not, bitch, I'll smoke you too. Ain't no love over here." He flared his nostrils. "Both of you bitches playin' wit' my freedom right now. Get me the fuck out of here. If I ain't out of dis ma'fucka within three months, man, on my mama, bitch, I'm going to the Feds. I'm going on yo' punk ass, Mudman, and on you Keisha. Bitch, one way or another, dey gon let me up out of dis ma'fucka. Mark my words." He stood up. "Both of you pussies quit looking all stupid. Get up and go make it happen. Y'all got three months. Give me my hug, Keisha."

Keisha glared up at him. "Nigga, fuck you." She stood up.

He yanked her to him and squeezed her ass, then tossed her backward before Mudman could jump up. As soon as he did, Payroll threw up his guards. "What, nigga? Fuck you wanna do? I can make dem calls today. Play wit' me."

Mudman grabbed Keisha and pulled her to him. "Yeah, a'ight, Payroll. I guess I'll be seeing you soon den."

"Betta be more sooner den later. Time is of the muthafuckin' essence." He turned his back to them. "Three months. That's all you got."

***

Figgady turned his Benz truck onto the busy intersection of Martin Luther King Drive. It was three o'clock in the afternoon and just starting to drizzle outside. He activated his windshield wipers and stepped on the gas. He was no more than a block on King Drive when he saw a red Chevy truck, pull to the curb and push Chela out of it. The truck sped away. Chela staggered and fixed a big red sweater over her shoulders. Then she was walking down the avenue. She was trying her best to walk as sexy as she could as if she was trying to catch a date.

Figgady furrowed his eyebrows. He was sure that she had never seen the truck he was driving before. He pulled the truck to the side of the curb and tapped the horn. He was sitting behind tints. He knew that she couldn't see him.

Chela walked up to the truck and knocked on the passenger's window glass. The rain began to head down as if a geyser had been broken. "Hey, you looking for a date?"

Figgady hurried to the back of the truck. He was at the back passenger door on her side. He yanked it open as fast as he could and grabbed her arm. "Chela! What the fuck you doing out here?"

Chela was so high that it took her a second to understand who the man was that was holding her. She was gone off of heroin and Oxycontin. She felt as if she was in another world. "Figgady?" She squinted her eyes. "Boy, let me go. I need to make me some money before I get sick later. I'm broke." She smelled rank. Her hair was nappy, and disheveled. Her clothes were way too big for her. She had on mascara, but it was all over her face.

Figgady opened the passenger's door. "Come on, Chela, you finna roll wit me for a minute."

"No, I ain't either. I'm finna make me some money. You not finna stop me from making what I need to keep my sick off." She jerked away from him.

Figgady grabbed her more firmly and slammed her to the truck. "Bitch, stop playin' wit' me." Lightning flashed across the sky. The rain beat so harshly that it felt like the pair was being attacked by hail.

Chela pushed at him. "I need to make sure I'm good for later. Get off of me! Help! Help! He tryna rape me! Help!" she screamed.

Figgady looked around. There were cars zipping past on the street. A few pedestrians walked across the road. When they made it to the other side, they looked back at them, seemingly concerned. "Shawty, stop dis shit."

"No, I won't stop it. You don't run me no more, Figgady. I'm my own woman." She yanked away from him.

He took a hold of her wrist. "Look, Chela, I got you, baby. Look at dis." He pulled out an ounce of Sinaloa. "Dat's dat good shit right there. You can have as much of it as you want. All I wanna do is to talk to you."

Chela straightened up. She pulled a tuft of her long curly hair behind her shoulders. "Okay, Figgady, let's go talk."

Chapter 19

Figgady felt sick to his stomach as he watched Chela slide the syringe into her inner forearm and push down on the feeder. She stopped and pulled the rope off of her arm. She dropped it to the floor and fed the rest of the drug into her system. She smiled as it coursed tough her.

"Why, shawty? Why you start doing dis shit?" he asked. He sat across from her on the couch.

Chela's eyes rolled into the back of her head. "Yo mans got me hooked on dis shit. When I ran away from you." She nodded out and leaned all the way forward, snoring loudly.

Figgady allowed her to nod for a second. Then he clapped his hands together to alert her. "Wake up."

Chela's eyes popped open. "Don't do that again, Figgady. You're ruining my high."

Figgady dismissed her. "Shawty, what are you talking about when you ran away from me?" he inquired.

"When I ran away from you the first time, I took me and Chiah to Prentice's house. He took us in. He let us stay wit' him for a few weeks, then he demanded that I pay him something. When I told him that I didn't have nothing to give him, that's when he fucked me against my will and forced this shit into my system. I been hooked ever since. He got mad when I couldn't tell him where Mudman and Keisha were. I guess he called himself taking it out on me and Chiah." She nodded out and began to snore.

Figgady's antennas went up. "Fuck you mean he took it out on you and my daughter? What he do to her?"

Chela groaned. "Please, Figgady, let me tell you all of dis shit at another time. I'm floating right now." She smacked her lips and began to scratch herself. The scent coming from her body was nearly unbearable.

Figgady stood up and clapped his hands together over and over. He knew that it was the worst thing you could do when a person was gone off of Sinaloa Tar. It affected their ability to enjoy the drug. He kept on clapping over and over again. "Bitch, what did he do to my daughter?"

"Stop it! Stop it! Stop it!" she screamed. "He whooped her a few times. He whooped my ass too though. He said he hated her. But every time he tore her up, we fought. Den he would screw me and give me some of dat good shit." She closed her eyes again.

"You let dis nigga beat on my baby?" Figgady was irate. He paced back and forth. He was so heated that he didn't know what to do. "Why you didn't leave when he hit her the first time? Did he have you locked up or something?"

Chela was in la-la land. She snored and drooled. Her cheek met her shoulder. At the same time, she continued to scratch herself, and was fully aware of the things that Figgady was saying to her.

Figgady walked over to her and slapped her as hard as he could. "Bitch, get up."

Chela opened her eyes. It took a second for what he'd done to kick on to her. "Ow! Why did you smack me?" she cried.

"Bitch, why didn't you leave when he put his hands on my daughter the first time?"

Chela curled her upper lip. "Nigga, dat's all you care about, ain't it? All you care about is Chiah. Didn't you hear me say that he took my body from me? He forced that poison into my system, and now I can't get enough of it."

"Bitch, you grown. Chiah is a baby. She can't stand for herself. You can. The minute he did something bogus with my kid, you was supposed to been up out of that house and back to me. You the reason all dis shit is happening." He was angrier.

160

Chela stood up. She nearly lost her balance, but then caught herself again. "You saying dat dis shit is my fault?" She pointed to herself.

Figgady nodded his head and stepped into her face. "If you had never left yo' monkey ass out of the house with my baby, she would be here right now. You so fuckin' stupid. I swear to God, I feel like whooping yo' ma'fuckin' ass right now."

Chela backed up. She looked around in a panic. "Figgady, if you even thank 'bout putting yo' hands on me, we gon' have a major problem. I ain't taking no more ass whoopings from nobody."

"Where is my daughter now? You gotta have some idea of where dis nigga is keeping her. Where is she?"

Chela shrugged her shoulders. "Don't know, and I ain't 'bout to stress myself out over it either. Figure since you worship the ground she walk on dat you would have found her by now," she spat.

"Fuck you say?" Figgady stepped closer to her.

Chela didn't back down. "You heard what I said. Since you care about him putting his hands on hurr, but you don't care about what he did to me, I wash my hands of it. You'll figure it out."

Figgady snapped. He swung as fast as he could. He wanted to knock Chela's head off of her body. He'd had enough.

Chela ducked and came out of her bra with a razor blade. She came up and sliced him three times across the face with blazing speed. Then she kicked him in the balls.

Figgady hollered and landed on top of the glass table. Glass popped into the air. "Arrgh! You bitch!"

Chela stood her ground. She was tired of running from men. She was tired of being victimized. She was ready to stand toe-to-toe with Figgady, even if it meant that he would beat her into the ground. "Get yo' ass up! Come on, Figgady!"

she screamed. She waited for him to begin to come to his feet. Then she jumped on his back and sliced him across the eyelids, before he flipped her on top of the shattered table.

Figgady felt the blade slice across his left eye. It hurt so bad that he screamed like a female. He fell back to his knees, holding his face. Blood gushed out of his wounds. He jumped to his feet to locate Chela.

Chela snatched the lamp from the table. She raised it over her heads and smashed it into the back of Figgady's skull. He fell again, dizzy. "Fuck you! I hate you, Figgady. You've always bullied me. You've always treated me like shit, and Chiah like a princess. Ahhhh!" She kicked him in the stomach, flipping him over. Chela bounced on her toes. She balled her hands into fists and held them under her chin like a boxer. She watched Figgady squirm.

Figgady stood up. Blood was dripping off of his face like paint. He caught sight of Chela. He felt nothing but hate. No longer did she register as his baby mother. She only registered as an enemy. She rushed him with the blade, and this time he was ready for her. He pulled his silenced .40 Glock and smacked her as hard as he could with it. He cracked the center of her forehead.

Chela flew backward. She landed against the wall. She slid down it and sat there for a second. The crack in the middle of her head leaked like a faucet. She got back to her feet. She wiped the blood away. "Dat's all you got, Figgady, huh? All dese years you been kicking my ass. Dat's all you got?" She rushed him, swinging wildly.

Figgady picked her up by the throat and slammed her down on the arm of the couch. Her neck snapped over the arm. She felt a pain shoot down her back. Her toes went numb for a second. The razor blade dropped from her hand. Figgady picked her back up and slung her over his shoulder. He carried her into the bathroom and threw her in the tub. She struggled to get up. He knelt down and punched her over and over as hard as he could. Blood continued to drip down his face. It looked like he'd stuck his head into a pot of red sauce.

Chela groaned over and over. She tried to fight him back. He took her head and slammed it against the faucet, dazing her. "Oof!" Was the only sound she could make as she sat in the basin, dazed.

Figgady stood up. He pulled the shower curtain around the tub. He mugged Chela with intense hatred. His left eye was stinging so bad that his knees were wobbling. He looked down on her and shook his head. All of their good times passed before his eyes. Then all of the bad. He remembered the night that she had given birth to Chiah. It had been the happiest day of his life. Then he came back to reality. He felt his own blood dripping down his neck. He thought about her being responsible for Chiah's disappearance, and it became too much.

Chela snapped out of her daze. She looked up to see Figgady aiming a silenced .40 Glock at her. She stared for a second, then screamed, pouncing up at him. She saw the bright flashes. She felt the first bullet hit her neck. Blood popped out of her. The second burned a hole through her cheek. It knocked her head back. She lost her balance. She looked up to see Figgady's angry snarl. Then she started to feel so many bullets hitting her back to back that it was impossible for her to feel the searing pain any longer. She faded out just as her brain oozed in front of her eyes.

Figgady stood back. He looked down on Chela and fell to the floor on his knees. He grabbed her by the hair and yanked her to him. "Damn, shawty. Fuck. You made me do dat shit. You made me do dis." He left the bathroom and came back with his tool kit. In the next twelve hours, he would be busy cutting her down to small enough pieces that the alligators would be able to consume them easily. His next stop was Prentice. The man had to answer for his daughter. He wanted his baby back. He refused to wait any longer.

***

Mars stepped into the pod and rubbernecked. It was Friday afternoon, the weekend of Labor Day, and he was sure that he wouldn't be able to see a judge until Tuesday. Sometimes the courts were so backed up in Oakland that it took twice as long to get a bail hearing as it did in other counties throughout the state. He held his bedroll under his arm. When he got to his bunk, he slung it on top of it.

Payroll saw him right away. He dropped the cards and hurried across the room. "Mars! Mars! What's good, my nigga?"

Mars smiled and met him in the middle of the room. They hugged and shook up. "Long time no see."

Payroll stood back. "Boy, what da fuck you doing in here? I thought you was out there getting money wit' Mudman."

"Aw. I was. Sheri got out of line. I had to fuck her up a li'l bit. She called the police, and, well, here I stand."

"Damn, that's a cold one, Cuz. But it's all good doe. You ain't gon' be in dis bitch for more than a few days. Come on. I'ma get you squared away. I wanna know everything that's taking place out there wit' Mudman. We finna most definitely chop it up."

"Cool, anything you wanna know, you already know I got you. My loyalties are to you first and foremost."

Payroll led him to the far end of the dorms, where they sat down. He motioned for the people sitting in that area to move around so they could have some peace and quiet. Once the area was clear, they took seats. "So, tell me. Is that fool out there getting money?"

"Hell yeah. He raking dat shit in the duffel bag now dat he fucking wit' The Bull. Every Friday we have money counting sessions. That nigga be having me counting money 'til I'm dizzy." He laughed. "He don't fuck wit' money counting machines either. He strictly want his shit counted by hand."

Payroll was already jealous. "What's the most you ever counted for him in a day?"

"Me personally? One million cash. That's about the norm."

"A million?" He was in disbelief. The most he had ever seen was two hundred thousand. He started to hate Mudman.

"Yeah, but you gotta remember that seventy percent of dat shit is going back to The Bull."

"Dat don't matter. If you counting a million in cash, and its other ma'fuckas in the room that's doing the same thing, sooner or later that thirty percent that he keeping between all of those duffels gon' add up to a million for him to take home. I mean, it's simple mathematics. How many other people be in the room counting that dough?"

"Da rest be all butt naked bitches."

"'Bout how many?"

"At least ten." Mars wiped his mouth and looked around the compacted room. There were prisoners walking around shirtless. They were buff, and a bunch of them were rivals. They mugged him and gave him stares that he was sure was meant to intimidate him. "Man, I know you got a piece for me?"

Payroll nodded. His slid his hand into the mattress and handed Mars an eight inch blade made out of the bed railing. He'd even managed to have it ridged. "You already know how I get down. Twelve ain't on shit in here either. They don't give a fuck what happens to a nigga. Been two murders last week in dem showers. I'm glad you here so you can really watch my back."

Mars looked up and saw the cameras. "What about dem?"

Payroll followed his line of vision. "Dem ma'fuckas don't work. Da ones by the shower don't either. Dat's why so many ma'fuckas been getting da bidness. One of their officers got hit up last week too, so now they on some fuck us type shit. Every man for dey self. I'ma be down here for a few days. I got court next Friday for dis child support shit."

Mars tucked his blade. "Dat's what's up."

"So, tell me somethin else about dis nigga? He a better leader den me?"

Mars shook his head. "You my day one. I'm still feeling bruh out. I will say dat he got us eating. He turned the projects around. He paying bills. He got them to rebuild the Boys and Girls Club. He paying li'l kids for bringing home A's and B's on their report cards. And he got the shooters and husslas eating. Ma'fuckas honoring Mudman, fa real."

Payroll nodded angrily. "You make dat nigga sound like Jesus to da ghetto a something."

"Nall, I just wanted to paint you a picture. But I'm saying, you already know I'm down for you. I can tell when you thinking somethin'. What you want me to do?"

Payroll laughed. "You already know I got a mission for you, don't you?"

Mars snickered. "How much bread does it entail, and when you want it done?"

Payroll was quiet for a long time. "You already know where his safe houses are, right?"

"Of course, I do. He treating me like his right hand man."

"And what about the combinations?"

"I'm the only one wit' him when he do 'em. I got the low down on his every move," Mars bragged.

"I figured you would." Payroll was excited. "Look, it's good that you had to make dis pit stop. We finna get all of our ducks in a row while we're together. Before they release you back to the street, we gon' have our shit on point. You wit' me?"

"Since we was fifteen. The floor is yours."

Hood Rich

Chapter 20

Figgady slumped lower in the seat of his stolen Chevy Caprice. He had a half of mask that covered his face. His big hands were encased in black leather gloves. He eyed Prentice's house with determination. He noticed that there were cameras on each of the posts that overlooked the yard. He had a bodyguard that paced in the yard as well. Figgady also noticed that there was a Mercedes Benz that drove around the block over and over. He guessed that Prentice had a crew of killas that was patrolling his house. He seemed to have his operation in order. Figgady knew from working close beside him that he was extremely intelligent when it came to the game of the streets.

Pistol held a Draco on his lap. He was hopped up off of Percocets and codeine. His entire face was covered by a ski mask. "What you thanking, Figgady?" He eyed the house and its white picket fence that Prentice was known to stay in.

Figgady looked at his watch. It read 3:10 in the morning. If he knew Prentice like he thought he did, he suspected the man to be inside knocked out. Prentice stayed high all day long. By the time two in the morning hit, his body was usually worn out. "I'm tryna see what's the best way to approach dis situation. He got a ma'fucka pacing back and forth in the yard. Nine times out of ten, he's armed. Then he got dese fuck boys doing rounds checking on his shit from dey car. We can't forget about them cameras either. Seem like its gon' be a bit of a task." Figgady eyed the house again.

Pistol shook his head. "Dat ma'fucka might have yo' seed in dat house. Anything could be wrong with her. I done been a part of her life since she was three years old, mane. Da way I see it, we go in there and make it happen. She been gone for six months, Figgady. Fuck is dis nigga doing wit' her?"

Figgady imagined some heinous acts. The visuals made him sick to his stomach. "Yeah, you right. Fuck it, let's handle dis bidness. First thangs first. We gotta holler at buddy that's pacing back and forth in the yard."

"Nigga, say no mo'." Pistol set the Draco on the back seat and pulled a silenced .40 caliber out of the console of the seat. He lowered himself as Prentice's detail rolled around onto the street to check on the status of the house. "Dese ma'fuckas been circling around every three minutes. Dat means I got three minutes to handle my bidness." The car rolled to the end of the block and made a left. As soon as they pulled off, Pistol opened the car door and slid out of the whip.

Figgady waited until he closed the door and pulled off in the car. "I'll be back."

Pistol nodded and crept low to the ground. He ran through Prentice's neighbor's gangway until he came to the backyard. Once there, he jogged to their garages and began to climb up it in the cover of the night. He checked constantly for Prentice's cameras. He located them and made sure he stayed clear of their view. He kept imagining Chiah's precious face. His heart was saddened. How could any man keep a kid held hostage for as long as Prentice had, he wondered?

When got on top of the garage, he low-crawled across the roof. His knees slid across the rough terrain. As he got to the edge that overlooked Prentice's yard, he pulled his .40 and looked over the edge.

Prentice's security was just making his way back toward the back of the house with a serious mug on his face. He kept his hand tucked inside of his fatigue jacket, on the ready. If anything looked out of the normal to him, Prentice told him to shoot first, and they'd figure out what was what later.

Pistol aimed his gun with one eye open and the other one closed. When he felt like he had his target locked in, he cocked back the hammer, and pulled the trigger three quick times. Foof! Foof! Foof!

Prentice's security caught two to the back and one through the shoulder. He turned around. Pistol finger-fucked his gun some more. He stood him straight up. The man flew backward and wound up on his side, bleeding out.

Pistol slowly slid back the way he had come and climbed back down the roof. He sent Figgady a quick text that said "It's done. Step two?"

***

Figgady picked up his phone and read the message. He set it back down on his passenger's seat. He was parked in the middle of the street slightly sideways, right at a stop sign. The Draco sat on his lap. He had a plan in mind. No matter what, he swore that he was getting his daughter back tonight. He looked in his rearview mirror as the car that had been doing its rounds turned onto the block. It rolled until it got in back of him. The driver expected him to pull off. He was blocking the narrow road. When he did not, the driver blew his horn.

Figgady ignored him. He slumped lower in the seat. His heart was racing a mile a minute. All he could think about was Chiah. He had to get her back.

The passenger jumped out with a .9 in his hand. The street was pitch dark with the exception of a streetlight a half a block backward.

"Say, mane, move dis busted-ass car. We need to get 'round yo' ass."

Figgady kept quiet. Once again, he slumped even lower. His knee was killing him. It felt like somebody was digging into it with a screwdriver. He knew he needed to seek medical treatment immediately.

The passenger threw his hands up at the driver. "Don't seem like nobody in that ma'fucka."

"Go see, nigga. Somethin' look crazy, pop they ass. Dis a one way street. You already know how Twelve is."

The passenger waved him off. "Yeah, a'ight, mane." He made his way closer to the car.

"Come on. Come on. A li'l closer. A little more," Figgady cooed.

The passenger got to the passenger's side and tapped on the glass. "Say, mane, move dis ma'fucka." He waited. He grew impatient. He looked closer and placed his hand in a sideways funnel to look inside of it. He looked right into the barrel of the Draco.

Figgady smiled and pulled the trigger, lighting up the car. The passenger was dead before he knew what was going on. Figgady jumped out the whip and ran full speed to the car in back of him. He limped and stopped as the driver tried to back out. Figgady let the Draco ride over and over. He wet the driver with twenty rounds. Shells tinked on the ground. He searched the car and confirmed that it had only been those two. "A'ight, Prentice. Nigga, here I come."

***

Pistol dropped into the tub of Prentice's bathroom. He was surprised at how the window had been carelessly left open for anybody to climb into. He guessed that Prentice wasn't expecting to be invaded. He had too big of a head. He was used to men being afraid of him, Pistol surmised. But he felt he needed to get a load of Chicago niggas. Pistol eased open the bathroom door with the barrel of his gun leading the way. He inched it open slowly but surely. When it was open far enough for him to stick his head out, he jumped back. The stench coming from inside of the house was so strong that he couldn't help gagging. He covered his mouth with one hand and entered into the hallway. The scent got stronger and stronger. The house had all of the lights on inside of it. He held his gun in front of him on high alert. When he got to the doorway of the kitchen, he stopped in his tracks and leaned over, covering his mouth. He looked back at the table to make sure that he hadn't been seeing things.

On top of the kitchen table was what Pistol assumed to be little Chiah's body. It was covered in maggots. They had eaten through the plastic that she was wrapped in. Behind her was the freezer that Prentice had kept her in for months. Pistol picked up his phone and called Figgady. He didn't know what else to do.

***

Prentice rolled past the Welcome to Oakland sign and stuck his face partway out of the window. He took a deep breath and inhaled the fresh air of the city. He had finally made it. He picked up his phone and read over the address once again that had been confirmed to be the place where both Keisha and Mudman were staying. He felt a cold chill go down his spine. He couldn't wait to enact his revenge. He couldn't wait to make them pay for what they had done to him. He vowed to make it the most sadistic murders that the world had ever seen. He stepped on the gas and headed to Cypress Village. "Yeah, muthafuckas, here I come!" he hollered out loud.

Behind him were two vans filled with his coldhearted hittas. They were dead set on turning Oakland out and making it the murder capital of the world before they were done with it. Mudman would have no idea what he was up against. The hatred in Prentice's heart would make sure of that.

***

Payroll hopped out of his bunk and grabbed his shower gear. He slapped Mars's bed and woke him up. "Say, homie, while dem ma'fuckas at rec, come watch my back so I can jump in dis water."

Mars sat up and nodded. "Yeah, a'ight, Loc, I got you." Mars grabbed his knife from under the bed and tucked it into his waistband. He followed Payroll into the shower area and got on point.

Payroll turned on the shower and disrobed. He stepped inside it and lathered up his body. "Yeah, homie, long as a ma'fucka stick to da script, we gon' be alright. I'ma make sure you eating like a ma'fucka. I done told you everything that I know about dat nigga and Keisha. That shit gold." He grabbed his shampoo and began washing his hair.

Mars felt a presence. He looked over his shoulder and saw two guards standing a short distance away from him. The dark-skinned Black one nodded his head while the Hispanic one closed the door to the shower room and stood in front of it.

Mars pulled the homemade knife from his belt and stepped into the shower behind Payroll while he was still going on and on about making him a Hood Legend. "All rats gotta die, nigga." He stabbed him in the back and proceeded to jug him over and over again.

Payroll fell face first into the shower. His kidneys had been pierced. He began bleeding through his penis almost immediately. "Mars, what the fuck? I thought you was my nigga."

"It's all about dat bag, nigga. Mudman got it. You old news. I murder him, and I'ma be the man. It's over." He stabbed him over a hundred times and slit his throat. He wiped the handle off of the shank and left it inside of the shower right next to Payroll's body.

***

Mudman got the call that Payroll had been taken care of. He snickered and slammed the duffel bag that was encased with a hundred thousand dollars on top of the table. He began to take the cash out stack by stack. Around the room were ten naked females counting his bag dollar for dollar. They sat at long tables side by side. Two armed killas from his project in Baton Rouge walked around on security. Mudman was responsible for paying all of their family's bills. He kept his killas eating until they burped. In exchange, they pledged their undying loyalty to him. He would have it no other way.

He looked around the room again and nodded his head at the success. He was starting to feel like a king. He felt that he had a long way to go, but the feeling was most definitely present.

"We up all night, ladies and gentlemen. Let's make dis shit happen," he ordered.

***

Prentice eased the Lexus truck to the curb. He pulled out his binoculars and watched Keisha take two grocery bags out of the trunk of her Benz. She handed them to Sandra. Sandra laughed and made her way into the house. Keisha grabbed three bags and followed Sandra into the house. She left her trunk open because there were five more bags in the trunk still.

Prentice slid his mask over his face and grabbed his .45. He slid from the truck, and stayed low as he could, thankful that the sun was beginning to set. When he was within fifty yards of the house, he took off running toward it with murder on his mind. He rushed up the steps and inside of the two-story house, catching both women off guard. Sandra screamed. Prentice raised his arm with his finger on the trigger, deadly revenge plaguing his mind.

To Be Continued...
Cartel Killaz 2
Coming Soon

Submission Guideline

Submit the first three chapters of your completed manuscript to ldpsubmissions@gmail.com, subject line: Your book's title. The manuscript must be in a .doc file and sent as an attachment. Document should be in Times New Roman, double spaced and in size 12 font. Also, provide your synopsis and full contact information. If sending multiple submissions, they must each be in a separate email.

Have a story but no way to send it electronically? You can still submit to LDP/Ca$h Presents. Send in the first three chapters, written or typed, of your completed manuscript to:

LDP: Submissions Dept
Po Box 870494
Mesquite, Tx 75187

DO NOT send original manuscript. Must be a duplicate.

Provide your synopsis and a cover letter containing your full contact information.

Thanks for considering LDP and Ca$h Presents.

Coming Soon from Lock Down Publications/Ca$h Presents

BOW DOWN TO MY GANGSTA

By **Ca$h**

TORN BETWEEN TWO

By **Coffee**

BLOOD STAINS OF A SHOTTA **III**

By **Jamaica**

STEADY MOBBIN **III**

By **Marcellus Allen**

BLOOD OF A BOSS **VI**

SHADOWS OF THE GAME II

By **Askari**

LOYAL TO THE GAME **IV**

By **T.J. & Jelissa**

A DOPEBOY'S PRAYER **II**

By **Eddie "Wolf" Lee**

IF LOVING YOU IS WRONG... **III**

By **Jelissa**

TRUE SAVAGE **VII**

MIDNIGHT CARTEL

DOPE BOY MAGIC

By **Chris Green**

BLAST FOR ME **III**

DUFFLE BAG CARTEL **IV**

HEARTLESS GOON **III**

By **Ghost**

A HUSTLER'S DECEIT III
KILL ZONE **II**
BAE BELONGS TO ME III
SOUL OF A MONSTER III
By **Aryanna**
THE COST OF LOYALTY **III**
By **Kweli**
THE SAVAGE LIFE II
By **J-Blunt**
KING OF NEW YORK V
COKE KINGS IV
BORN HEARTLESS II
By **T.J. Edwards**
GORILLAZ IN THE BAY IV
De'Kari
THE STREETS ARE CALLING II
Duquie Wilson
KINGPIN KILLAZ IV
STREET KINGS III
PAID IN BLOOD III
CARTEL KILLAZ III
Hood Rich
SINS OF A HUSTLA II
ASAD
TRIGGADALE III
Elijah R. Freeman
KINGZ OF THE GAME IV

Playa Ray

SLAUGHTER GANG IV

RUTHLESS HEART II

By Willie Slaughter

THE HEART OF A SAVAGE II

By Jibril Williams

FUK SHYT II

By Blakk Diamond

THE DOPEMAN'S BODYGAURD II

By Tranay Adams

TRAP GOD II

By Troublesome

YAYO II

A SHOOTER'S AMBITION II

By S. Allen

GHOST MOB

Stilloan Robinson

KINGPIN DREAMS

By Paper Boi Rari

CREAM

By Yolanda Moore

SON OF A DOPE FIEND II

By Renta

FOREVER GANGSTA

By Adrian Dulan

LOYALTY AIN'T PROMISED

By Keith Williams

THE PRICE YOU PAY FOR LOVE
By Destiny Skai
THE LIFE OF A HOOD STAR
By Rashia Wilson

Available Now

RESTRAINING ORDER **I & II**
By **CA$H & Coffee**
LOVE KNOWS NO BOUNDARIES **I II & III**
By **Coffee**
RAISED AS A GOON I, II, III & IV
BRED BY THE SLUMS I, II, III
BLAST FOR ME I & II
ROTTEN TO THE CORE I II III
A BRONX TALE I, II, III
DUFFEL BAG CARTEL I II III
HEARTLESS GOON
A SAVAGE DOPEBOY
HEARTLESS GOON I II
By **Ghost**
LAY IT DOWN **I & II**
LAST OF A DYING BREED
BLOOD STAINS OF A SHOTTA I & II
By **Jamaica**
LOYAL TO THE GAME
LOYAL TO THE GAME II

LOYAL TO THE GAME III

LIFE OF SIN I, II III

By **TJ & Jelissa**

BLOODY COMMAS I & II

SKI MASK CARTEL I II & III

KING OF NEW YORK I II,III IV

RISE TO POWER I II III

COKE KINGS I II III

BORN HEARTLESS

By **T.J. Edwards**

IF LOVING HIM IS WRONG…I & II

LOVE ME EVEN WHEN IT HURTS I II III

By **Jelissa**

WHEN THE STREETS CLAP BACK I & II III

By **Jibril Williams**

A DISTINGUISHED THUG STOLE MY HEART I II & III

LOVE SHOULDN'T HURT I II III IV

RENEGADE BOYS I II III IV

By **Meesha**

A GANGSTER'S CODE I &, II III

A GANGSTER'S SYN I II III

THE SAVAGE LIFE

By J-Blunt

PUSH IT TO THE LIMIT

By **Bre' Hayes**

BLOOD OF A BOSS **I, II, III, IV, V**

SHADOWS OF THE GAME

By **Askari**

THE STREETS BLEED MURDER **I, II & III**

THE HEART OF A GANGSTA I II& III

By **Jerry Jackson**

CUM FOR ME

CUM FOR ME 2

CUM FOR ME 3

CUM FOR ME 4

CUM FOR ME 5

An **LDP Erotica Collaboration**

BRIDE OF A HUSTLA **I II & II**

THE FETTI GIRLS **I, II& III**

CORRUPTED BY A GANGSTA I, II III, IV

BLINDED BY HIS LOVE

By **Destiny Skai**

WHEN A GOOD GIRL GOES BAD

By **Adrienne**

THE COST OF LOYALTY I II

By Kweli

A GANGSTER'S REVENGE **I II III & IV**

THE BOSS MAN'S DAUGHTERS

THE BOSS MAN'S DAUGHTERS II

THE BOSSMAN'S DAUGHTERS III

THE BOSSMAN'S DAUGHTERS IV

THE BOSS MAN'S DAUGHTERS **V**

A SAVAGE LOVE **I & II**

BAE BELONGS TO ME I II

A HUSTLER'S DECEIT I, II, III

WHAT BAD BITCHES DO I, II, III

SOUL OF A MONSTER I II

KILL ZONE

By **Aryanna**

A KINGPIN'S AMBITON

A KINGPIN'S AMBITION **II**

I MURDER FOR THE DOUGH

By **Ambitious**

TRUE SAVAGE

TRUE SAVAGE II

TRUE SAVAGE **III**

TRUE SAVAGE **IV**

TRUE SAVAGE **V**

TRUE SAVAGE **VI**

By **Chris Green**

A DOPEBOY'S PRAYER

By **Eddie "Wolf" Lee**

THE KING CARTEL **I, II & III**

By **Frank Gresham**

THESE NIGGAS AIN'T LOYAL **I, II & III**

By **Nikki Tee**

GANGSTA SHYT **I II &III**

By **CATO**

THE ULTIMATE BETRAYAL

By **Phoenix**

BOSS'N UP **I , II & III**

By **Royal Nicole**

I LOVE YOU TO DEATH

By Destiny J

I RIDE FOR MY HITTA

I STILL RIDE FOR MY HITTA

By **Misty Holt**

LOVE & CHASIN' PAPER

By **Qay Crockett**

TO DIE IN VAIN

SINS OF A HUSTLA

By **ASAD**

BROOKLYN HUSTLAZ

By **Boogsy Morina**

BROOKLYN ON LOCK I & II

By **Sonovia**

GANGSTA CITY

By **Teddy Duke**

A DRUG KING AND HIS DIAMOND I & II III

A DOPEMAN'S RICHES

HER MAN, MINE'S TOO I, II

CASH MONEY HO'S

By Nicole Goosby

TRAPHOUSE KING **I II & III**

KINGPIN KILLAZ I II III

STREET KINGS I II

PAID IN BLOOD **I II**

CARTEL KILLAZ I II

By **Hood Rich**

LIPSTICK KILLAH **I, II, III**

CRIME OF PASSION I & II

By **Mimi**

STEADY MOBBN' **I, II, III**

By **Marcellus Allen**

WHO SHOT YA **I, II, III**

SON OF A DOPE FIEND

Renta

GORILLAZ IN THE BAY **I II III**

DE'KARI

TRIGGADALE I II

Elijah R. Freeman

GOD BLESS THE TRAPPERS I, II, III

THESE SCANDALOUS STREETS I, II, III

FEAR MY GANGSTA I, II, III

THESE STREETS DON'T LOVE NOBODY I, II

BURY ME A G I, II, III, IV, V

A GANGSTA'S EMPIRE I, II, III, IV

THE DOPEMAN'S BODYGAURD

Tranay Adams

THE STREETS ARE CALLING

Duquie Wilson

MARRIED TO A BOSS... I II III

By Destiny Skai & Chris Green

KINGZ OF THE GAME I II III

Playa Ray

SLAUGHTER GANG I II III

RUTHLESS HEART

By Willie Slaughter

THE HEART OF A SAVAGE

By Jibril Williams

FUK SHYT

By Blakk Diamond

DON'T F#CK WITH MY HEART I II

By Linnea

ADDICTED TO THE DRAMA I II III

By Jamila

YAYO

A SHOOTER'S AMBITION

By S. Allen

TRAP GOD

By Troublesome

BOOKS BY LDP'S CEO, CA$H

TRUST IN NO MAN

TRUST IN NO MAN 2

TRUST IN NO MAN 3

BONDED BY BLOOD

SHORTY GOT A THUG

THUGS CRY

THUGS CRY 2

THUGS CRY 3

TRUST NO BITCH

TRUST NO BITCH 2

TRUST NO BITCH 3

TIL MY CASKET DROPS

RESTRAINING ORDER

RESTRAINING ORDER 2

IN LOVE WITH A CONVICT

Coming Soon

BONDED BY BLOOD 2

BOW DOWN TO MY GANGSTA